D1095191

OP 5ᵃᶜ

PASSERMAN'S HOLLOW

Books by Jane Stuart

WHITE BARN
(poems)

YELLOWHAWK
(a novel)

A YEAR'S HARVEST
(poems)

EYES OF THE MOLE
(poems)

PASSERMAN'S HOLLOW by JANE STUART

McGRAW-HILL BOOK COMPANY
New York   St. Louis   San Francisco
Düsseldorf London Mexico Sydney Toronto

Copyright © 1974 by Jane Stuart.
All rights reserved.
Printed in the United States of America.
No part of this publication may be reproduced, stored in a retrieval
system, or transmitted, in any form or by any means, electronic,
mechanical, photocopying, recording, or otherwise, without the prior
written permission of the publisher.

23456789 BPBP 7987654

Library of Congress Cataloging in Publication Data

Stuart, Jane.
    Passerman's hollow.

    I. Title.
PZ4.S927Pas [PS3569.T82]   813'.5'4   73-15816
ISBN 0-07-062202-7

For Conrad and Erik

How art thou fallen from heaven,
O Lucifer, son of the morning!
ISAIAH 14:12

PASSERMAN'S HOLLOW

He awakened thinking of Carla. Her violet blue eyes followed him as he turned on the bed and stuffed his head under the striped ticking pillow. Red and white, blue and white, colors to dream on at night. Up through the feathers came the haziness of those violet-blue eyes, swimming in circles of springtime lavender. Flower petals that opened and closed, closed and opened, giving only snatches of their smile before they closed themselves off from him, wilted and went away. Lost themselves.

He reached for her eyes. He tried to touch them. His hands, cupped nervously beneath his puffed-up cheeks, jerked back and forth clumsily when the petals opened. His long bony fingers, raw from recent scratches and sore from the naked skin that had festered, jabbed away when the eyes opened and stared at him from far away, safe in their sacred distance.

"Carla," he whispered, frightened. "Carla, please."

The eyes wrinkled and the thin, delicate lids, lined with tiny purple veins, fell to cover the glistening pupils—then he could almost make out her smile, a soft-lipped, open smile, her mouth turning up unexpectedly at the corner tips. Yes, it was almost her smile, he thought with an ache as his voice cracked down into his chest, his courage crumpled, and he lay there, heart throbbing, chest aching, his lower body surging, all of him mastered, humiliated, overcome by the damp eyes and knowing smile.

Then, reluctantly, he stretched out his long body and wiped his hands on the corner of his plaid wool blanket; he lay there on the rollaway, trembling, his body worn out from the passion that the image had dragged out of him. It was worse than spending a night with the devil, these dreams of Carla. It took more out of him than he could build up by work or sleep, it drained him of all the strength he took in from the quiet understanding looks of his family.

Downstairs he could hear pans being knocked against each other as they were pulled out of wood cabinets and down from unlined shelves. His mom was up, probably Rebecca, too. He lay there quietly, trying to stop his breathing, hoping to enter into their morning world and overhear their words. But there was no sound; they were so quiet. His heart pressed down against the rollaway, his ear against the ticking pillow, he could hear the quick, light, easy steps of Rebecca making a checkerboard of red crossing with the black heaviness of his mom's slower moves. From stove to refrigerator, from refrigerator to stove to cabinet to unlined drawer—in his mind he could see the oilcloth being wiped off by Rebecca, little Rebecca brandishing an old dishrag; then the plates and coffee cups would go down, the forks and knives be laid out, the spoon holder set in the middle of it all with a thud. He smelled flour and grease and a hot, thick, cooking smell —drop biscuits and oatmeal and link sausage.

He drifted off to sleep again and then the kitchen door swung open and heavy boots sounded on the linoleum floor, stamping off the coagulated snow and dirt and twigs that had stuck to their worn-down, size-10 soles.

"A thaw's coming," the deep, fierce voice of his father announced. It was early morning and his father spoke in an early-morning voice. No sweetness for his mom or Rebecca, no softness for the boy who lay asleep on the rollaway upstairs. It was a tough, hard winter voice, his pa's voice, and there was no way to disguise it. It was a voice that crooned to cows as they dropped their calves, a voice that called down fighting roosters, a voice that yelled "timber" as giant hands and rusty saw felled a sick tree. It was the voice of a man who feared God and knew that the next life would bring peace and plenty to those who had prayed and worked on earth, all those God-fearing men who had taken their lot in life and made the best of it, never complaining over sickness or death or hunger or poorness or even more the things they could not understand, the mysterious things that the hand of God sometimes wrought.

"A thaw!" The boy could see his mom's eyes, bright, blue, turning up to meet her husband's with quick understanding, hurt, and fear. "A thaw! When?"

"Too soon." The harsh voice was gruff and strained, but no softer.

No one said a word. The boy drifted and was again awakened by a thin clash against the floor, then another, and another. Clink, clash, clink, clash, queer metallic sounds that told the boy that the milking was done. His father had set down one pail, Griffith and Bristol unloaded one each. Poor boys with so much work to do. He didn't really care so much about Bristol having to work, but Griffith was just a baby. A big eight-year-old baby in snow booties and a lace-trimmed, blue wool cap. He giggled. Then he stopped when he heard a muffled grunt as Rebecca lifted up the pails one by one and set them on the sink board, heaving up the tin with all her might so that she could strain out the milk.

"Help your sister," his father said to one of the boys, and the door slammed to again. They're on the stoop, Ruben thought, raising himself a half inch from his bed, heaving himself up quiet like a cat, tiptoeing across the floor on boards that he knew would creak if he let down his full weight. He waited until he was sure no sound had leaked down, then leaned against the wall, arching his thin trembling body as he pushed his head down against the boarded-up spot that used to be a window. He knew from times before where there was a crack. He pushed his ear against it, held it there, and breathing slowly, carefully, stopped his heart from pumping so loud he could not hear.

"When'll it come?" he heard his mother ask. She was still thinking of the thaw.

"Within the week."

"Something will have to be done."

"That's the gospel truth."

Arise therefore and be doing, and the Lord be with thee, Pa.

He could hear Rebecca pouring the milk through pieces of washed-out cheesecloth into the metal cans.

"Who'll take care of it?"

"I will."

"You can't manage alone."

"I'll have to." (God takes care of them who help themselves, his pa was thinking.)

"I can help. Or Bristol."

"Bristol?" his father laughed and thought of his idle-minded, golden-haired boy. "You don't really think he knows?" Bristol lived in a world that shut out ice and snow, a world that waited for summer's dog days when he could wade the sluggish creek waters and watch dragon-flies sleeping in the air. Bristol wouldn't take the time to know anything that didn't interest him. And Ruben's doings didn't interest him at all.

"Yes, he knows."

"Who told him?"

"No one had to, with his brother shut up in a room upstairs."

"Maybe so. But I don't think Bristol knows as much as he lets on. He's just feeling you out." Bristol, his golden-haired son, the joy of his days, the hope of his prayers. Bristol knew nothing but that the days and nights were the handiwork of God and the firmament of His creation, his mother and father were there to be honored, God was to be praised above all men, and life was a thing for thanksgiving not to be coveted but taken with a happy grain of salt because within the flashing of an eye or the sounding of a trumpet it could disappear, be called back to the Maker who in His mercy had given it to be used for His glory. Bristol, child of his father, for whom it had been written ". . . from a child thou has known the holy scriptures, which are able to make thee wise unto salvation through faith which is in Christ Jesus."

The mother said nothing. Ruben could picture her tired hands folded in her apron, her lips pursed together, waiting.

"We'll see," his father repeated.

"All right. But if you don't take Bristol, I'm going. The others can look after Ruben."

"No. We've got to get Ruben out of here."

"I won't hear to it." His mother's voice had grown cold and certain, the way Ruben knew it got when she was asserting herself. She was the true mother who looked Solomon in the eye and said, This is my son. She knew how to call a bluff.

"We'll talk about it later. But I say Ruben has got to go."

"No."

The door slammed to. Winter threatened the kitchen and then the heavy sound of boots being pulled loose and scraped against the flat, sharp-edged rocks to pull off the caked mud told the boy that more than winter was threatening.

"Pa's going back in," Ruben whispered to himself. "He'll be up for me." He scurried back to his rollaway, tiptoeing lightly like a squirrel on two delicate feet, nuzzling down into the rollaway. He pretended to be asleep.

The sound of a key turning in the lock. Under the plaid blanket Ruben grinned. Does he really think that old lock works? he wondered. Doesn't he know I could pick it with my little finger if I wanted to be out of here in no time?

Yes, he knows, came a little voice inside his head. He knows. But where would you go? He knows that, too. He knows you have no place to go.

Not true, Ruben answered himself, gritting his teeth to make his answer more biting. Wicked, nasty devil, answering him, questioning him. Not so, I could go lots of places.

The little voice laughed and Ruben's head throbbed from

its laughter. Then the laughter melted away, flowing from the ugly, eddying, gurgling sound into the light, spring-green laughter of Carla.

"Go away," Ruben shouted hoarsely. "Go away, I don't want to hear you." He picked up the pillow and pulled it down over his head. He pressed its ticking hard against his hair, letting the sweat that was beading up on his scalp run against the red and blue striping of the case and wet the sharp-edged feathers that were pricking their way through.

"Go away, go away." He let himself collapse into sobs that shook his body and the rollaway. Then, thrashing from left to right on the narrow bed, he wrapped himself into a cocoon, pinning the blanket tightly beneath his chin, pressing the pillow down over his muffled face.

"Go away," he sobbed into the goose feathers, "go away."

"It's only me," Pa said.

Silence. Stillness. Ruben lay quietly in his little nest, pretending sleep. The violet eyes were gone, the curled-up smile, the girlish laughter.

"It's only me, Rube," Pa repeated. "I've come for you."

Ruben thrust out one naked hand. He pulled at the sweat-soaked blanket and struck aside the pillow.

"Pa?"

"Yes?"

"I must of been dreaming. I must of had a nightmare."

"I guess you did, son."

"I can't imagine why I've had bad dreams, though, can you, Pa?"

For a dream cometh through the multitude of business; and a fool's voice is known by multitude of words.

No, the man said at last.

"Is it late, Pa? Have I slept late?"

"It's almost seven."

"I've slept a long time."

"It's all right, boy. Sleeping's good for you. But you're bound to be hungry now. I've come to take you to breakfast."

"I'm not hungry, Pa. Do I have to come down?"

"Yes."

And there are times when you must do what the Lord tells you to do and not what you would do yourself. Ruben sat up slowly and propped himself on the side of the bed as he reached for his clothes. He pulled on the jeans and socks and underpants laid neatly across his chair. He grabbed his boots by their tops and plugged his feet inside them, pulling up the carved, Western, leather sides with the tips of his fingers. Then he groped for his shirt.

"I brought you a clean one, boy," his Pa said. He opened the door, letting in some light, and handed Ruben the freshly washed and ironed shirt hanging from the doorsill. Then he set in a pan of water, washrag, soap and a towel. "I'll wait for you in the hall."

"Can I have some light, Pa?"

"I'll leave the door cracked."

Ruben washed himself slowly, savoring the feel of luke-warm water against his bare skin and the slick bar of rough soap sliding up and down his body. He rubbed hard to clean off the dirt and sweat and smell from his shoulders and stomach. His hands stung as the soap seeped into their cuts, but Ruben worked on, cleansing his body as best he could.

"You about through?" his pa asked from the hall.

"Coming."

The boy moved sideways to the door, sticking his head through first. Then he slithered out. His father walked behind him down the steps, guiding him into the kitchen. There his family was already seated at the long table, sipping coffee with milk as they buttered their hot bread.

"Good morning," his mom said. She did not move to kiss him.

Ruben nodded shyly.

"Aren't you going to speak to your mother?" his pa asked.

"Morning, Mom."

He nodded to Rebecca and Bristol and Griffith. They

spoke back, Rebecca with her mouth half full and her head turned away as she got up to pour his coffee.

Ruben sat down at the empty place between his mom and dad. He took heartily from the biscuits and sausage and oatmeal.

"I'm hungry after all, I guess," he told his father. "It seems like days since I've had anything to eat. I don't guess that's right, though. Is it?"

Feed the hungry, clothe the naked.

His father and mother looked at each other, then at him.

"No, Ruben," Rebecca said, swishing past him with a plate of leftovers for the dogs. "You ate like you was starved last night."

"Where you going, Becky?" the boy followed his yellow-haired sister's movements sorrowfully. "You going away and leave me?"

"I'm giving this to your hounds, Ruben," she said. "Can't you hear them hollering? I can't stand to eat with them not fed."

Ruben let out his breath and turned to his full plate. He picked up his fork and spoon again and began to cut his sausage into little pieces. They don't think I've noticed about the knife, he thought. But I have. I know they won't let me have one.

And the Assyrian stood up and took the knife and with its sharp blade smote down the Babylonian. There was something wrong about that, but it had come from the Bible, hadn't it, and it meant death to the unbeliever, the heretic, the man who had defied God and His firmament of stars and trees and green planted wonders. After all, *Who is a liar but he that denieth that Jesus is the Christ? He is antichrist that denieth the Father and the Son.*

"What are we going to do today, Pa?" Bristol asked, shaking his golden head as he smiled up at his father.

"Fence mending," the father answered him absentmindedly.

"Has there been a break? I thought the fences were in

good shape. Why, Ruben just checked them . . ." his voice hollowed out.

Ruben, stalling a bite of sausage that was traveling to his mouth, looked up with a smile. "I know where you're going," he said. "To the north meadow. Isn't that right? Down by Passerman's Hollow? Isn't that where the cows have been breaking out?"

"That's right, boy," Pa told him.

"Are you going to take me to help?"

"No, Rube. Your mother needs you here."

Ruben turned to his mother. "What are we going to do today, Mom?" he asked her, parroting the question Bristol had asked his father. His smile was simple, but his eyes were razor edged. "If it's quilting or mending or helping Becky with the house cleaning, I just may go back to bed." Throwing down his fork and spoon with a clatter, he glared at them all defiantly.

There was silence. No sound of fork-scraped plate or coffee being slurped from its cup onto the saucer to drip down on the oilcloth.

"If I can't help mend the fences in the north meadow," he went on angrily, feeling the sausage in his stomach rise up and growl at the fried eggs, feeling his face go purple and his eyes bulge red, "I won't help at all."

"Ruben," his pa said heavily, "Ruben, you can't go to the north meadow."

"I knew it!" the boy screamed, half to himself, half to them all. "I knew it! I knew you wouldn't let me go. Ohhhhhhh," he groaned, and slumped forward.

His mom caught him up under one arm and his pa under the other. They lifted him firmly from the chair and walked him up the stairs. His mom, just a woman looking old and tired before her time from growing unsure of God's purpose, put the boy back to bed and covered him with his blanket. The father, grim and knowing that some men must bear the burdens of others who were too weak to shoulder them, stood waiting for her in the hall, then watched her pick up the pan of water and soap and carry it out quickly. Then he locked the door and faced his wife.

"God punishes," he said firmly. "Ruben has to go."

"But where?"

"I don't know."

"For how long?"

"I don't know that, either."

"Who'll look after him?"

The father shrugged.

"I won't have my son out alone. He's queer but he's my firstborn."

What, my son? And what, the son of my womb? And what, the son of my vows?

"You have two other sons to look out for. And a growing daughter. A daughter who's almost a young woman," he added thoughtfully. "It's not like you had only the one child. You have four. And every one of them is dear to me."

"Except that one." She nodded to the boy in the room.

"No, including that one. Maybe that one more than the others, because he needs all the love I can give him. And because he's got none to give back. I pray to God to help me make the right decision about him—I pray every day and every night—"

Then she grabbed the big arm in her small firm hand. "The decision has been made, husband," she snapped. "And we'll stand by it."

He looked at her and knew defeat. A mother bird will protect its young, he thought. No matter what or why. "God's will be done," he muttered, bowing his head.

"God's will is being done," she hissed back.

"It's different to you, he's a boy . . ."

Her bright blue eyes hollowed him down to the size of a child that she was reprimanding.

"It's no different," she said. "If it were Rebecca in there . . . if it were Rebecca, why we'd do the same thing. Do you hear me?"

Ruben's father stared through her and nodded. "But it

wouldn't be Rebecca," he said softly. "It couldn't be Rebecca."

"Why couldn't it? I never thought it would be Ruben. But it is. It's my son. My child, my God-fearing child . . ." Her voice, quiet from whispering, grew hoarse with emotion. Her hand with the pan of dirty water trembled and sloshed some out on the floor. "And it could be my daughter, husband. Remember that."

"Little Rebecca," the man crooned. "Just a little girl with yellow hair . . . and your blue eyes . . ."

"You yourself just told me that Rebecca's almost a grown woman. Maybe you're the one who'd better remember it."

They stood facing each other in confusion, striking out like angry, coiled-up snakes that attack each other because there is no one else to strike at; because there would never be anyone else to confide in, anyone to tell them if they had done the right thing or if they would die in the fires of hell because they had sinned against the holy writ of the God they loved. Their faces, lean and pulled from the strain of uncertainty and fear, seemed tortured shadows to the boy peering at them through the crack in the wall.

"What are you going to do with him today?"

"I don't know. I'll think of something. I always do."

They heard a noise and turned to the stairs. Rebecca stood there, her eyes on her feet, ashamed of what she had heard but shaken by a fright so strong that it made her stay and wait until the quarreling was through.

"What is it?" her mom asked, bending down.

"A car," she whispered, gesturing to Ruben's room with her finger held warningly to her lips. "A car."

Rebecca, clearing off the table and scraping dishes into a pail for the hogs, had heard the motor coming from a distance. She could tell from its struggle that a car was chugging down the valley road, and her heart inside her blue print dress contracted.

"Why do I feel that way, now?" she asked herself. "There's no trouble in a car crossing the valley road. Nothing to get so worked up about. Lots of cars go by in the daytime, some at night."

But the car did not stop or turn off on a side road. It began to cough and sputter its way up the hill, sloshing through mud and spitting snow that ground away underneath the tires in an effort to hold it back. Three times it stalled, three times Rebecca's heart relaxed and then went into spasms again as she heard the motor whirr loudly, angrily, and the wheels spin and clutch at the churning earth beneath them. Once a door slammed, a man cursed aloud and, as his voice cracked the air, the wheels spun again and the car cranked forward.

"There's two of them," Rebecca caught herself stopping to think. "One's got out to push. Maybe they're stuck. They've got to be stuck. Maybe they can't get out. And maybe they'll stay there forever," she prayed to the tired car of the God she had borrowed from those who needed Him more, for just a moment, just to listen to her plea.

But the car swore and spun and came on.

At what she guessed was the entrance to the north meadow, a mile or two from Passerman's Hollow, Rebecca heard the car stop. She smiled, relieved, said Thank you, God, although she knew she shouldn't have, and went on about her work of pouring the cream back into a jar, covering it with a saucer and setting it in the refrigerator; firming the pat of butter; dumping out the morning's coffee grounds. She poured a little dish of milk for the cat and patted his lean black flanks.

"I'm glad they've stopped," she told the cat and herself. "They're just visitors down there."

She took out a fresh dish towel, one she had embroidered with "Monday," even though it was the end of the week, and dried the glasses she had rinsed off. As she was stacking them, rims down, on the shelf she was always planning to line with newspaper but still hadn't taken the time to do, she heard the car start up again.

"O, Lord," she felt her insides turning upside down. "O, Lord, they are coming here."

Beads of golden sweat stuck to her fine, flat-combed hair. She brushed off her forehead with a sudsy hand and forced herself to walk to the steps. Up there, on the landing, her mom and dad were talking in low shaky voices. Maybe Ruben's heard them, she thought, and not the car. Oh, how she hoped he'd not heard the car.

Her mom hurried down the stairs and took her back to the kitchen. She plunged her hands into the dishwater and made a racket with the pans. Rebecca explained, as well as she could over the noise, how she had followed the sounds of the car from the valley road until now.

Her father stood alone, leaning against the edge of the front-room window, looking down at the hill. His eyes were clear and hard as they made out the form of the car, now muddied and grimy and dripping with sediment as it wheezed its way up the hill.

"It's a blue Ford truck," he said. "One man's driving and two are pushing. It'll be a while before they get here. Rebecca," he turned to his daughter, handing her the key to Ruben's room, "get Rube and take him to the barn. Have him help Griffith and Bristol clean out the stalls. Tell the boys to keep an eye on him. Tell them not to let him come in."

The girl went at once up the pine steps for her brother.

Ruben was standing at the open door, grinning, when she reached for his hand.

"Come on," she whispered. "We've got to go out to the barn."

"I heard a car," Ruben said.

"I know."

"Do you know who it is?"

"No. Pa says it's a blue pickup with three men."

"The sheriff, I'll bet." Ruben grinned. "He's got the prettiest little blue pickup I ever saw."

"Come on, Ruben."

The boy looked her over challengingly. "I'm not afraid."

"I know you're not. Neither am I. But come on."

"Who says to?"

"Pa."

"I won't go."

"Mom?"

"No."

"For me, Ruben?"

The boy stuck out his trembling hand and stroked his sister's silky hair. Then he smiled and slipped his hand into hers. "All right, Becky," he said. "I'll go with you."

Rebecca led him down the steps and out the kitchen door. She stopped twice, once to button up the jacket she had brought along for Ruben, the second time to pick up the pails of hog slop she had set out on the stoop. The pails were heavy and her shoulders hurt when she carried them. Ruben watched her strain for a moment, then reached out to her with a happy smile. "I'll take one," he said.

Bristol and Griffith were leaning on their pitchforks listening to the noise of the stalling engine when they saw Ruben and Rebecca coming down the path. Baby Griffith looked older holding a pitchfork but Bristol was the same, pink cherub face and gold silk hair flying loose in the cold. Dreaming of summer and dog days, bare feet in cool creek water, hands ready to trap a water moccasin with a forked stick. Damn Bristol. No, love thy brother.

"What do you suppose is up?" Bristol asked.

"Some sort of trouble, I reckon," Griffith told him, thinking of the car. "Let's go help Becky."

They came to take the slop pail from their sister and help her scuddle her way through the heavy frosted slime that had oozed across the path. Rebecca had no need of help, she walked surefootedly, but her ankles slipped when they turned in the deep cow's tracks that were hidden beneath the ice-giving-way-to-mud and her left shoulder drooped from the weight of the slop pail.

"Pa says you're all three to work out here in the stalls awhile," she said meaningfully. "And not to come in till he calls you."

"Sheriff's coming," Ruben said simply.

Bristol and Rebecca and Griffith looked at each other. Then Rebecca shrugged her shoulders and said, "He knows everything that happens."

Ruben grinned shyly at his sister. "I'm not so dumb, am I, Becky?"

"No, Ruben, you're smart," she told him. "You're not dumb at all."

"Look, Ruben," Bristol said, as he helped his brother over the plank spanning the muddy ditch into the barn. Don't you worry about nothing. We'll just do as Pa said for us to."

"Sheriff's coming," Ruben repeated.

Rebecca led Ruben on through the whitewashed barn and out the back doors, down the path to the hog pen. They carried one pail of slop between them.

"What can we do?" Griffith asked, leaning his pitchfork in the empty stall. "Pa says he's not to have anything sharp around him. Says he might hurt himself."

"That's right," Bristol said. "We'd better lock all the tools up."

16

"Maybe we could work at bridging this mud a little better."

Griffith shook his head. "Pa says there'll be a thaw."

Bristol nodded. "Soon."

Griffith looked at his older brother oddly, saw him standing there dreaming in a world of his own, and said, "Bristol, I think maybe we ought to do something that really is work. So it won't look just like we're covering something up. Let's shovel out the cow stalls. I don't see how Ruben could hurt himself that way."

"All right."

Bristol stood shifting from foot to foot and looking first towards the house, then back at the hog pen, while Griffith climbed into the loft to hide their pitchforks under a pile of hay. Then Griffith came down and the boys went back of the old wooden wagon that their pa kept standing inside the barn and took out the shovels that they stored there under the harness that had belonged to old Bessie, their grandpa's horse, the horse that had pulled the wagon when Pa was just a little boy.

"Dig in," Bristol said, coming to suddenly as a gust of cold wind hit him in the face.

Griffith, who could hear the truck grunting as it came closer up the hill, picked up his shovel and lowered it into the litter that cluttered the stall's floor. When Pa was a boy and Grandpa was just a pa, he thought to himself, I wonder if these things went on. But he didn't really think so, because there weren't many pickup trucks then, and people didn't venture out in them in the wintertime when the roads were bad and folks had work to do taking care of their land and looking after their own.

Crystal Gilbert was a big man who drove his wife crazy eating cheese sandwiches and drinking buttermilk. No matter what the time of day or year, he wanted his buttermilk fresh-churned and cold and waiting for him in the refrigerator, and he liked to have a box of Velveeta cheese right there beside it and a loaf of sandwich bread ("white or wheat, it don't matter, Velvet, just so it's there, you know a man as big as me gets hungry, sweetheart"). He wore heavy overalls, a blue workshirt and warm lumberjacket. Although it was still the dead of winter, he wore no hat or gloves and his neck was rough and scaly where the sun shone down on it and snow and rain and wind had beat against it. He was a big mountain man, a good sheriff, and a father who knew his county's children as well as he knew the back of his knotty hand. Now he took his time parking his little blue pickup in the driveway of the Lawson's farmhouse. He sat for a moment behind the wheel, letting the motor run to warm him up while he finished the cheese sandwich his wife Velvet had sent along with him to hold him over until he could get home for lunch, thinking to himself while he munched the flabby cheese and soft bread. Then he folded the wax paper neatly so Velvet could use it again, put it in the glove compartment where he kept a cigar or two in case he felt the need to smoke, opened up the door of the pickup and walked slowly through the slush to the front porch of the house where Mason Lawson and his wife Hilda lived with their four children.

When she heard a knocking at last on the door, Hilda wiped her hands on her apron and called out, "Who's there?"

"Crystal Gilbert, Cousin Hilda," the big voice boomed. Every woman was cousin to Crystal who kept on friendly terms with everyone in the county and always kept an eye open towards election day.

Hilda turned to her husband. Mason Lawson nodded towards the door.

"Come in," she called, "and have a cup of coffee with us."

"I'll do that."

As she listened to him pulling off his muddy boots on her doorstep, Hilda's heart throbbed hard in her chest and her bright slitted eyes squinted at her husband, scrutinizing his passive face carefully and threateningly.

"Good morning." Mason Lawson rose from his cane chair and held out one large red hand. Crystal Gilbert took it and pumped it a long moment, weighing the firmness and strength and steadiness in the five fingers and cool palm.

"Good morning, Mason," Crystal said at last. "Nice to see you, Mrs. Mason."

Under her breath, Hilda smiled at his old-fashionedness. "You're early this morning," she said with a nod as she set down a clean cup. "Just in time for breakfast."

"I can see you've eaten," Gilbert told her, having taken in the empty table when he first came in the room.

"That we have," Mason said. "We move early here. But there's still some cold biscuits and Hilda's preserves if you've a mind to try them."

Gilbert smiled. "No one can set a glass of jelly like you, Mrs. Mason," he said. "If I didn't have my men waiting in the yard, I'd take some."

"Ask them in," Mason said politely.

"No, thanks, they're cleaning the mud off this old truck of ours," Crystal told him. "You've sure got a thaw coming up this way, Mason. The ice is giving way fast. I saw two streams of water starting to trickle down the hill as I came up."

"Is that so?"

"Yes. I reckon you and your boys will make the rounds for damage?"

"We're planning to start today."

"Any place in particular you're going?"

"No," Mason Lawson said carefully. "We'll just follow the fence and see if any posts have started to give way."

"That's a good idea," Crystal Gilbert agreed. "A good idea. Well, you can afford to take your time and check it out slowly with those three boys to help you."

"Yes."

"How are they?"

"They're fine."

"Let's see . . . Griffith, Bristol, and Ruben. Right?"

"That's right."

"And how's the girl?"

"Rebecca?" Hilda asked. "She gets prettier by the day."

"I can see that," the sheriff said as the door opened and Rebecca came in smiling, her face flushed pink from the chilly air, her long yellow hair flying loosely around her shoulders.

"Good morning, Mr. Gilbert," Rebecca said.

"Hello, little lady. You're up and about early this morning."

Rebecca smiled. "Spring is on its way," she said. "I'm having to hurry to beat it this year."

The sheriff laughed. "Just like my Rosie," he said. "Out looking for the first violets before the snow's gone!"

Rebecca laughed with him, trying to make a natural sound follow the way he had said "violet," the way he had made a delicate word sound crude and common when he wheezed it out in his gutteral voice that smelled of cheese and suspicion.

"Well, you're right, Mrs. Mason, the girl does get prettier each time I see her," Crystal said, pouring more cream into his half-empty cup as Rebecca left the room. "I'd say she's the prettiest girl on East Fork now. I guess she always was, really."

"Rebecca has more than looks, praise the Lord," Hilda Lawson said steadily. "She's a good cook and seamstress and a God-fearing girl."

"I believe that," Crystal Gilbert smiled. "I always thought that she and Carla Adkins were the finest young women around here."

Hilda looked at the sheriff firmly, fastening her bright blue eyes on his ruddy face. "What news of Carla?" she asked. "We're sick with grief about the girl here. Grief and fear. We've four of our own, you know."

"I know, Mrs. Mason. If I were the mother of such a daughter as yours, I'd be frightened, too. What's been going on around here is enough to chill the souls of good people like you."

Mason Lawson shivered in his seat, twisting his big hands in his lap. "We don't talk much about it," he said quietly. "Carla was Rebecca's best friend, you know. And the only near one she had. And you know how the boys felt about her. They were all close."

"She was like another daughter," Hilda said.

"Her being an only child, I'm sure she appreciated having a large family close to her," Crystal said. "But you asked what news there's been. None. Dear God, not a trace of her. A week gone by, and not a trace."

"Any clues, Mr. Gilbert?"

"Clues? Mason, there's always clues. People always have ideas and suspicions and crazy notions in their heads that a thing like this gives them a chance to let out." Crystal stretched his long legs and rubbed his shoed-in feet against each other. "I hear tales about ghosts and runaway horses and people going mad and killing the girl. One letter I got said it was from a good friend who'd seen her running away. I've had phone calls from people in Clayton and MacPherson who swear they've seen her clerking in stores there. I make the ride over and check the story out. But no Carla.

"I tell you, Mason, I'm stumped. I don't know which way to turn. I've made this run up this hill, over these meadows, down the lanes, under the trees—I've checked out every place I could think of, I've investigated every living person around here—but I can't come up with a single thing! It's about to drive me crazy. And the girl's parents. Dear God, they've given up. They just sit in that house and stare at the walls. Have you been over lately, Mrs. Mason?"

"I was there day before yesterday," Hilda replied. "And our Rebecca is going this morning with some bread and soup."

"Glad to hear that. They need all the company they can get from folks like you who won't inquire and upset them with snooping around."

"We wouldn't do that." Mason sat looking towards the fire and Hilda stood behind him, looking down towards her large red boned hands, wondering where Rebecca had gone off to and how much she had heard said about Carla.

"Well," Crystal pulled himself up, and started fastening his jacket. "Well, I'd better get on, Cousin Hilda." He beamed about him. "I just dropped in for a chat and a cup of coffee. I started early this morning—thought I could beat the roads tearing up. But no luck. All I found was mud."

"Come back," Mason said, standing up.

"Oh, I'll come back," Crystal smiled. "I'll be back. Say . . ." he turned around and looked through the house. "Where's the boys?"

"They're in the barn lot."

"Got them at the chores already, huh?"

"Yes."

"Mind if I go out and say hello to them?"

"Not at all. Let me go with you. It's time I got back to work. That barn lot's in bad shape, but I guess it'll be getting worse with the weather that's on the way."

The door closed behind them. As Crystal Gilbert bent over to pull on his boots, his words were carried away by the wind. Hilda Lawson stood watching them with Rebecca suddenly at her side. The two men, talking loudly, came around the side of the house and started down the path to the barn.

"I've done the upstairs rooms, Ma," Rebecca said.

Her mother nodded blankly, her eyes on the three figure shadows bobbling up and down at the barn, up and down as they shoveled and straightened up to toss their load of litter into the bed of the old farm truck that now replaced the wagon used by Grandpa Lawson long ago.

Once he had got there, Crystal didn't really have much to say to the boys. Just a friendly grin, some showoff shadow boxing against the side of the barn and a few tips on how to make the shoveling easier. The boys, standing straddle-legged in the heaped-up stalls, grinned their approval of his near-champion swings and grunted in response to his suggestions. Sweat was pouring down their heads and their hair was slicked to their faces like it had been starched by a Quaker family.

"Good workers you've got here, Mason," the sheriff smiled. "Maybe someday I can hire one or two of them on as deputies. Not that being a deputy is an exciting job—but it might beat cleaning out a barn."

The boys laughed.

"I'd like to be your deputy, Mr. Gilbert," Ruben said then, eyeing the sheriff from behind his loaded shovel. "I'd make you a good one."

Crystal Gilbert regarded the boy thoughtfully. "I imagine you would, Ruben," he said. "I'll remember your offer."

"Thanks."

"Well, I must be off." The big man thrust out his hand to Mason Lawson. Once again, the men exchanged a firm steady grip. Then, moving very quickly, Gilbert turned on his heel and held out his hand to Bristol, who was still leaning against the handle of his shovel.

"Good to see you, Bristol."

Surprised, the boy took the man's big hand in his bare one and pumped it.

"You, too, Griffith."

Griffith leaned across the stall and gave the sheriff his little hand and a big smile.

"Ruben?"

"Yes, sir?" The boy straightened up and eyed the sheriff. "I just dropped the shovel," he said. "I guess you wouldn't be wanting to shake my hand." He held up his hands, covered with mud and dung.

"No," Crystal Gilbert said. "I don't guess so."

He smiled at Ruben, then turned and walked away.

23

III

"**C**ome on now, boys," Mason Lawson said to Bristol and Griffith as he turned from watching the sheriff's big body retreat into his snow-shiny pickup. "I want you with me."

The two boys put aside their crudded shovels and wiped their hands on a feed sack slung over the loft stairs. They stamped and scraped their boots, swinging their arms to free the tension and cramping brought on by the heavy shoveling, letting the last drops of sweat run down their noses and fall into the snow.

"How about Ruben?"

"Not him," Mason said. He looked at Ruben with a firm hard eye. "Not him. You take him back to the house, Griffith. Bristol, get out the digger, a coil of wire, pliers and some nails."

A sly grin flashed across Ruben's sultry face. His eyes twinkled as they regarded his father's nervous coldness.

"Going fencing?" Ruben asked coyly.

"That's what I said this morning," Mason told him. "And I've not changed my mind."

Ruben grinned.

"Take him back, Griffith," Mason ordered his youngest son.

"Yes, Pa."

"Right now."

"Yes, Pa."

"I'll go myself," Ruben cried out in sudden anger, picking up his feet and leaping the wide, mud-ridged moat of dung and dirt and cattle tracks rimming the barn.

"Ruben!" Mason Lawson shouted. "Ruben, come back here!"

With a wild laugh that the wind carried away to hide, the boy darted off zigzag through the mire, his preened toes touching only the dry solid spots along the path that acted like a magnet to his cowboy boots. Griffith shook his head, watching his brother dance away like a dervish. Then he picked up the digger and smiled at his pa.

His jaw twitching, his Adam's apple bobbing, his heart throbbing, but without saying a word, Mason led his two boys across the field, following along the well-strung-out fence line. Silently and studiously they tapped each post to make sure that it was set firm in the ground. If in doubt, Mason made a test of placing his weight against the post and pushing. The boys, too small and light for this heavy work, checked the long strips of barbed wire. It was taut and sharp, sometimes with little tufts of cattle's hair clinging to the prongs. Griffith, for something to do, swung haphazardly at the nails anchoring the wire, hammering them harder, deeper, stronger.

"Things here look good, Pa," Bristol said.

"They do," Mason agreed.

"How far do we need to go?"

"Just a little more. I want to make sure there's no soft ground here . . . no danger of an artesian spring. Could be dangerous, you know. A cow could turn its hoof and fall . . . even break a leg."

Bristol and Griffith looked at each other, wondering who had put ideas of an artesian well into their pa's head. But Mason walked on, carrying the digger, tapping fence posts and looking carefully over his broad, wide fields. Once he dropped to his knees and pushed his hands against a raised mound of lumpy earth. "Moles," he muttered, shaking his head. He patted the earth back in place, his fingers testing for broken cracks.

"There's a lot of land here," Mason said. "An awful lot."

"Sure is," Bristol panted, wrestling with his coil of wire.

"I wonder how long it'll take us to check the fences this spring."

Griffith dropped to a rock and stared down into his sack of nails. "Weeks," he mumbled.

"You're probably right." He looked at the faces of his two sons. Their tired smiles and heavy eyes reminded him that it was Saturday, and there were games the boys would like to be playing and their own Saturday things that needed doing.

"All right, we might as well go on home," he said.

The boys broke into a run, yelling and whooping and suddenly full of themselves again. It was at times like this, when Mason Lawson watched his golden-haired Bristol sprint through the wind with Griffith at his heels, that Mason wished he were young again and could start life over. And then he caught himself, abashed, and stopped his thinking, suddenly embarrassed before the Lord.

It's vain of me to think of starting again, he realized as he stood in the cold wind repenting. I must be grateful for what I've learned and not think I could do any better. Without the Lord's help, where would I be? But then he thought of Hilda and Ruben, their firstborn, and the other three, and he could not but wonder to himself Why, Lord, Why? With or without Your help, is this what I'm to be? He thought again of Hilda and Ruben, of yellow-haired Becky, of Bristol and Griffith lost in their Saturday world, and offering a smile that did little to hide his bitterness up to the Lord, he walked on back to the house.

When Rebecca went to take the loaf of bread and half-gallon jar of homemade vegetable soup to Myra and Phace Adkins, she saw Crystal Gilbert's little blue pickup parked out behind the smokehouse. Crystal and Phace were walking, smoking and talking together. The two deputies were once again scraping loose mud from underneath the truck.

Rebecca knocked on the front door, and then walked on in. She found Myra Adkins sitting in the living room in her little gooseneck rocker, her face turned to the wall. An old doll of Carla's was on her lap.

"Good morning, Mrs. Adkins," Rebecca said. All of a

sudden her yellow hair crawled against her neck, her throat hurt, her chest ached. But she made herself repeat the words. "Good morning, Mrs. Adkins." Then she closed her eyes so she would not have to look at the doll.

Mrs. Adkins spoke her name without turning around. She's heard me here so often, playing with Carla, Rebecca thought, that she knows my footsteps. The girl shuddered, and went on talking to the starched back of the rocking woman.

"Mom sent me over with some fresh bread and soup. We made the soup yesterday and figured you'd like some. So I've fixed it up in a jar for you. It'll make you a fine lunch. Would you like for me to heat it for you?"

The woman raised her hand, and Rebecca fell silent. She stood there uncertainly, waiting to be given a signal if she was to leave.

"Rebecca," Mrs. Adkins said at last, a long and drawn-out word, very sad and very tired. "Rebecca. Did you come here alone?"

"Yes, maam."

"Your mom let you?"

"Yes, maam."

"She sent none of the boys with you?"

"No. They're busy with the barn and fences."

"They shouldn't be too busy to keep an eye on their only sister."

Rebecca shifted her feet uncomfortably and mumbled a quiet yes, maam.

"My girl's gone, you know."

"Yes, I know."

"Disappeared."

"Yes."

"They say she's run away."

"I know."

"Do you think she did?"

"I don't know."

"Do you think she'd run away from a good home and a mom and dad who loved her so?"

"I don't—"

"You know she wouldn't."

Rebecca said nothing.

"Come sit by me, here, on this stool."

Rebecca set down the soup and bread and went slowly across the room and sat down where she was told.

"What are they saying at school?"

The girl bowed her head, so she would not have to look into the grief-wrinkled face of the woman who rocked and looked at the wall as if it were a friend who knew and understood. "They don't talk much."

"What do they say?" Her voice shook with anger, then gave way to fear.

"They don't think Carla ran away."

"No." The woman relaxed and leaned her head back against the rim of the chair. "Neither do I."

"The principal told us not to talk about it," Rebecca said quietly.

"But you do?"

"Yes, of course."

"What do they say?" Myra Adkins asked again.

"They say—" Rebecca's voice trembled with something she did not understand. "They say that something—awful—must have happened to Carla."

"Do you know what they mean by that?"

"Yes, I think so."

"Then you shouldn't come walking here alone."

"Yes."

"Have your brother bring you next time."

"I will."

"Tell me . . ." Myra Adkins looked down on the yellow hair of the girl squatting at her feet on the sewing stool. "Tell me again about the last time you saw Carla."

Squinting her eyes so that the room fell into a blur and

she focused on nothing, and holding her hands very still on her crossed legs, Rebecca lifted her head and chanted in a singsong voice, "Last Friday, Carla and I left school together and walked to the bus stand. We were talking about our homework and the history test that was coming up Monday. Then Carla remembered that she'd left her book in the locker. She asked me to save her place in line. I did. She was back in about ten minutes, running and out of breath. Her face was flushed. She said she was sorry she'd been so long, but that she met someone in the hall and stopped to talk."

"Did she tell you who it was who'd stopped her?"

"No."

"Go on."

"We got on the bus and sat down together. Carla put her book in her satchel and started giggling."

"What was funny?"

"I don't know. Carla was always laughing. Things were funny to her."

"What was there in life that a thirteen-year-old girl couldn't enjoy?" the mother said to herself. "What could she have known then that would have frightened her?"

"We laughed and joked on the way home," Rebecca went on. "We didn't study any, the way we'd planned."

"What did you laugh about?"

"About . . . about what Carla had found funny," Rebecca said, puzzling over her own thoughts. "I teased her and tried to get her to tell me. But she wouldn't. She said, 'I'll tell you tomorrow, when you come over to study with me.'

"I said, 'Oh, you come over to my house, Carla. I went to yours the last time.' But she said, 'No, it's quieter at home. I don't have three brothers who make a lot of noise.' Then she started giggling. She was still laughing when the bus stopped at the foot of the hill and we started home."

"And how was it you came home?"

"Up the road together. Then Carla took the shortcut and I came on by the road."

"You didn't talk on the way up?"

"No. It's a steep climb. We saved our breath."

"And you never saw Carla again?"

"No."

"I did," the mother said half to herself, half to Rebecca. Now it was her turn to tell the story she and Rebecca had exchanged so often during the past week. "Carla came home. She was tired and hot and happy. She put her books in her room and helped me with supper. She told me about the test on Monday, and asked if it was all right for you to come here on Saturday to study with her. I told her, Sure. She said, 'Mom, it's my turn to go to Rebecca's, but it's quieter here. And we have a big test to study for.' I told her, 'It's all right, honey. You know your dad and I don't mind.'"

Then Myra Adkins stopped and drew her breath. "What day is it, Rebecca?" she asked, absently.

"Saturday."

"A week ago today, you were to have been here. Just you and Carla, two pretty little girls with yellow hair, sitting on Carla's bed and studying and laughing together. My, my." And Myra Adkins began to rock again.

"Please go on, Carla's mother," Rebecca said gently, hugging her knees together and remembering.

"Oh, yes. Well, Carla's dad came in at five-thirty and we ate our supper. We had cornbread and chicken. Isn't it funny, that I can remember that? No, it's not strange, I've gone over things so often in my mind. Then Carla and I stacked the dishes in the sink and changed clothes for church. Carla put on a pretty blue dress. It was her daddy's favorite.

"We went to church. We sat down on the pew next to your mom and dad. We weren't too late, just the way we'd planned. We were right on time for Friday-night church. After the hymns were sung, all the children went to the basement. What was it you were having?"

"A birthday party. A surprise party for Carla."

"She didn't know about it, did she?"

"No."

"But I knew. I knew about the cake and ice cream. I knew about the present her Sunday School class had got her. A zippered notebook. I was so excited. I sat on the edge of the pew, and listened for the laughter and the giggling. Her daddy knew, too. I think he was listening."

Myra Adkins turned over her hands and covered up her face. "Tell me what happened."

"I don't know, Mrs. Adkins," Rebecca said softly, aware that she was letting the woman down. But Myra Adkins sat on as if suspended, waiting to hear what had happened to her daughter, waiting for the story to be finished and maybe even for Carla to come jumping out from behind a closed door and cry, "Surprise!" She even covered her eyes so she would not spoil Carla's little game by peeking and seeing her too soon.

"I don't know what happened, Mrs. Adkins," Rebecca repeated. "Mom and Dad took Bristol and Griffith and Ruben and me to church early. You must have heard the car go by."

Mrs. Adkins nodded.

"We were there early, and the boys and I went to the basement. Some of the other kids from Fancy Creek were already there. We hung the streamers and put out the paper plates and napkins. And we waited for you all to come. We hoped you wouldn't get there too early, so Carla wouldn't come on down and see what we were doing."

"No. We didn't. We came just when your teacher said to."

"That's right. We heard your car pull up. We heard you come in and sit down. We heard the hymns begin. "Rock of Ages" was the first. Then the rest of the children, the ones from the other classes, got up and came downstairs. We waited for Carla. We waited and waited and waited."

"But she never came?"

"No, Mrs. Adkins. She never came."

"Oh, dear God in Heaven," Myra Adkins said as she began to cry. "She never came."

Sitting quietly at the kitchen table, listening to the conversation in the front room, Crystal Gilbert and Phace Adkins paid close attention to the story told by Rebecca and Myra Adkins. Crystal sat bent forward, his grisly red hair drooped down over his cupped hands. Phace was tall, solemn, warrior straight in his hard-back chair. The two men followed each word exchanged between mother and girl.

"I just don't know," Crystal Gilbert said, shaking his head. "I just don't know. I can't figure it. Can you, Phace?"

The father stared blankly at the wall.

"I just can't figure it. This is the third time I've heard that girl's story. And I've talked to the mother God knows how many times. But it doesn't click. It's a wrong lead. The girl doesn't know what happened to your daughter, Phace. Take my word for it, she's as innocent as I am. All that girl knows is that her best friend didn't show up for her own birthday party, and she sat in the basement and cried until church was over and she could come up and see what had happened."

Phace Adkins stared hard, biting his lips.

"I give up," Crystal Gilbert whispered, raising himself from the chair. "I'm going back to town and see what I can dig up someplace else. I'm sorry, Phace, but this just isn't any help. It's wasting my time and trying you and your wife's sanity to go over and over it."

Like a claw, Phace Adkins' hand shot out and gripped the rough red paw of the sheriff. "Mark my word," he said, and his own words were short and clipped and angry. "Mark my word, there's been monkey business. I'm a man who's sure of his own wife and daughter. But nobody else. Understand?"

"I understand, Phace. But don't be so hard on that girl. Just because—" and the sheriff chose his words as carefully as he could. "Just because she's a beautiful young girl who's still alive instead of your own daughter."

Phace Adkins looked the sheriff hard in the eye. "So you know Carla's dead."

Crystal shrugged his shoulders. "I don't know anything, Phace," he sighed. "But I'm making a reasonable guess. Isn't that what you think?"

"You know it is."

"And you know I'm doing everything I can, Phace?"

"You better be, Sheriff," the man said, shaking his head numbly from side to side. "You better be. Cause if I get to whoever did this first . . ."

"Then I'll be after you, Phace," Crystal said softly.

"I reckon you will." And Phace Adkins spat angrily into the kitchen fire.

IV

Ruben grinned and crooned to himself happily, clutching his big bare feet in his hands and swaying himself back and forth. The force of his body, rocking on the bed, caused the floor to vibrate and shook the ceiling of the kitchen, where Rebecca was stirring up cornbread for supper.

Shaking her head, the girl dusted the meal off her hands and crept up the stairs. What was he up to now?

"Oooooo," Ruben crooned, raising his voice high enough for Rebecca to hear. "Oooooo." He tickled his feet with his index finger, and started giggling. The more he tickled, the more he giggled. Rebecca, standing at the door, smiled and started to slip away.

Ruben, hearing the floorboards creak, became alert. She's leaving, he thought. She's going back downstairs and leaving me up here alone. I don't want to be alone.

He jumped to the floor, landing on the balls of his feet. Slouching over, he dropped his hands in front of his toes and dragged himself, like an animal, to the door.

"Little Becky's in the hall," he sang. "Little Becky came up to see if Ruben is all right. If Ruben is happy." And he began to laugh. "I hear you, Becky," he whispered. "I hear you. Speak to me."

"I'm here," his sister said.

"But you're leaving?"

"I have to go downstairs, Ruben. I have to start supper."

"Let Mom start it," the boy said petulantly. "I want you to stay here with me. I'm lonely."

"Mom's outside with Pa," Rebecca said.

"Where's Bristol?"

"He's out."

Run, Bristol, run. Shake off sorrow and run in the wind

while there is time. Silver and gold have I none, but such as I have, give I thee.

"And Griffith?"

"Him, too."

God bless the little children.

"Let me out, little Becky. Let me come and sit in the kitchen with you. I can help. You know I can."

"I'm not supposed to."

"I'll wash the dishes for you."

"Pa said not to," Becky said, her voice wavering.

"Woooooo," Ruben moaned, dragging himself about the room. "Wooooo." He picked the lock and opened the door. "Wooooo."

Then Becky began to laugh. "You're a sight, Ruben," she said. "What would Pa say if he knew you could do this?"

"He'd go 'Woooo,'" Ruben said, imitating the way his pa would stand up straight and look horrified.

Becky laughed again.

"You won't tell, will you?" the boy asked, plucking at her sleeve.

"No."

"You won't tell?"

"No, Ruben, you know I won't."

"Why? Why, Becky?" His eyes sought out hers and penetrated through the soft blue roundness beneath her freckled forehead.

"Why should I? I like to know you can go and come as you like. Besides, you're company for me when they're all outside."

"Hahahaha. Little sister gets lonely."

"I do, Ruben."

"Since—" and the boy leaned far over the threshold, balancing himself with his toes curled over the floor ridging, "since your little friend's gone, huh?"

"That's right."

"I'm sorry about your friend, Becky."

"Let's don't talk about it, Ruben."

"If you don't want to. We won't. I don't like for you to look sad." And Ruben stuck his fingers in his mouth and made a face, to show Becky how she looked when she was sad.

"You're a sight," Ruben," his sister grinned. Then she saw the scratched, raw hands held to his face. "Hasn't Mom been putting salve on them?" she asked.

Ruben took his hands out and turned them over carefully. He stuck them out for Becky to look at, turning them in, turning them out, turning them over and over as if he were tanning them and wanted every portion to receive the same amount of sunlight.

But when raw flesh appeareth in him, he shall be unclean.

"No," he said, his face suddenly becoming serious. "Mom hasn't been caring for them. She won't touch them. But I scrub them with soap."

Rebecca shook her head. "You need some salve. I'll go get it."

One long finger hooked itself around her wrist.

"You come back?" the boy asked.

"Yes, Ruben."

"Where you going?"

"Just down the hall. To Mom's room, where the salve and cloths are."

"Can I come?" The boy looked excited, as if it were a grand adventure Rebecca were taking. He wanted to come with her. His face was flushed, his hands were trembling at his sides, his bare feet were twitching.

"Sure," Rebecca said, looking at her brother and hurting all over for him. "But we'd better hurry. I've got to get supper on."

Rebecca took him by the hand and hurried down the narrow, pine-floored hall. Ruben reminded her of a little

37

child, hiding behind her skirts and peeking out when she said he could. She pushed open the door of her parent's bedroom and went in. He didn't follow. She turned to face him and found him standing there, quiet and smiling. He was waiting to be invited in.

"Come on," she said.

Then Ruben followed her, edging along the side of the wall as if he were trying to blend himself into the wallpaper. He walked like a shadow.

"I don't want them to see me," he told Rebecca, jerking his head toward the outside world. "They could, you know, through the windows there."

"All right."

Rebecca understood!

He watched her as she took a small jar from their mother's chest of drawers and a torn-off cloth out of the sewing basket.

"I've got what I need," she whispered to him, quiet and smiling, keeping the secret of their adventure. "Let's go."

But Ruben was looking at the bed. It was a large walnut, four-poster bed spread neatly with a hand-pieced quilt. The big double bolster was puffed up high, encased in a starched embroidered cover. On one side the pillow read "I slept and dreamed that life was beauty"; on the other side it said "I woke and learned that life was duty."

"Let's go."

But Ruben was looking at the bed. "Pretty," he said, squatting down on his haunches and half-crawling, half-walking towards the bed. "Pretty." He stroked the quilt, and fingered the bolster.

Rebecca tapped him lightly on the back. "We'd better go, Ruben. They may be back anytime."

"No." Ruben turned to her sharply. His eyes were brimming with tears. "No, I want to stay here. Just for a minute. You fix me here." And he climbed up on the bed.

"All right. But don't mess it up. They'll know you've been in here."

Ruben hunched his back and leaped lightly up on the bed. He turned carefully and sat facing Rebecca, his feet hanging over, swinging back and forth against the siding. He watched his feet for a while, then he leaned his head back and watched their shadows dancing on the ceiling.

"This room's haunted," he said at last, poking at Rebecca with a long pointing finger. "See up there?"

"Silly, it's just the shadows of your feet."

Ruben stared down at his bare swinging feet. "So it is," he said. "I have magic feet. They can dance on the ceiling when they're really on the floor."

Rebecca giggled and reached for his hands. He stretched one out shyly. "Don't hurt me," he begged.

"No, I won't, Ruben."

Gently, she rubbed the thick salve on the torn, raw parts of the boy's hand. She covered the crevices between his fingers, the worn-down cuticle at his nails, the scraped knuckles. Then she wrapped a cloth around it and laid it gently in the boy's lap.

"Give me the other," she said.

Ruben gave her his right hand, which she dressed as carefully as the other.

"Sometimes," the boy said, putting his mouth close to her ear, "sometimes they hurt a lot."

"I know they do."

"How do you know?"

"Once I went through a briar patch and scratched my hands and face," Rebecca told him, as she helped him down from the bed. "I was in poison ivy, too, so I had to take a bath and use Mom's strong soap. Oh, did it hurt. My skin cracked. It opened up. Little blisters came. It stung awful before Mom put the salve on me."

"I wasn't in a briar patch," Ruben said simply.

"No."

"And I didn't go through poison ivy."

"No."

"How did I hurt my hands, Becky?"

"I don't know, Ruben." She puffed up the bed and led her brother back to his room.

While he was waiting for supper, Ruben slithered back and forth on his rollaway and made tents with the blanket by thrusting up one knee. He held his bandaged hands beneath the cover and pretended he was a wounded Indian, being summoned into his chief's tepee to be commended for bravery in action.

"White Feather," the chief said, "you are a good brave."

Ruben bowed his head in respect.

"You have shown your pride and courage in war; you have used good sense and good judgment in governing your people well. Your fields have prospered. Your wives have born many sons. You have much grain stored away for the winter."

Ruben, as White Feather, turned his eyes inward and examined his fine, strong, brown body, his slicked-back black hair, his black Indian eyes, high cheekbones, the soft deerskin clothing he was wearing. Then again he bowed his head in reverence to the great chief's words.

"I have brought you here to tell you that your deeds do not go unnoticed. You have shown your skill as man and leader; and in the race today, you have won this symbol of accomplishment." The chief reached for a long, scarlet feather to tuck into the bonnet of the brave White Feather.

"Hold out your hands, my son, to receive your prize."

Ruben stretched out his arms, almost touching the walls of his blanket tent.

The chief remained immobile.

He did not give him his prize.

Ruben stared at the chief, then at himself. What was wrong?

"Your hands," the chief said. "How have you wounded yourself?"

Ruben held up his hands and looked them over carefully. He shook his head and then he answered, "Oh, Chief, I do not know."

The chief pulled his blanket about his shoulders and puffed away on his long clay pipe. His black eyes regarded White Feather coolly. "A wounded brave?" he said. "A wounded brave with the dressings of a white man? What treachery is this? You are a spy! You spy for the white man!"

"No, no," Ruben gasped. "No, I am Indian, I am war brave, I am White Feather."

The chief turned his head, muttered something, and two scouts came to drag White Feather away.

Outside the tent, the women turned upon him their silent, stony, black-eyed stares. The other braves spat, and then gave him their backs. The children ran away and would not come to him as they had before, when he called.

He heard the chief say from his tent: "Burn him."

Sweating, fear and horror on his face, Ruben sat up and the tent collapsed. He held up his hands and stared at them. "No," he whispered. "No, I deserve the feather. The prize is mine. I earned it."

Then he heard the little voice inside him laughing. He heard Carla's spring-green laughter join in. The laughter of the two voices grew louder, more mocking, driving out the image of the Indians, their camp, and White Feather standing bravely at the stake, ready to suffer, ready to die by torture.

"Go away," Ruben begged. "Go away."

He put his hands across his ears and dived beneath the pillow. But the laughter grew louder, since he no longer had the room's solidness to protect him, and he had revealed himself and his fear to the specters inhabiting him.

"Go away," he pleaded. Now he could see Carla, a swatch of purple cloud standing in front of the darker vibrations of his voice.

"Go away." He snapped at them, rolling his eyes and chomping his teeth together. He bit the pillow, the blanket, the bandages, his leg—he kicked and tore at the air in the room. But they only laughed and watched him.

Exhausted, then, he lay back down and turned his frozen stare up at the ceiling. There the purple cloud began to disintegrate and left in its place two violet eyes, watching him impudently from their distance.

"Please go away," Ruben whispered, "I won't bother you if you'll just go away."

The eyes blinked and two tears appeared at their black-lashed corners. The tears grew larger, larger and crystal hard, and round. Ruben could see himself reflected in their clearness. He saw his wretched, frightened face, his bandaged hands, his body squirming with fear beneath the blanket.

Ruben, sobbing, begged them not to fall on him.

But the violet eyes blinked, and the tears, gaining momentum, crashed down and exploded in his face. Their fury smashed against the walls and the room was suddenly filled with dozens of Rubens, dozens of frightened faces and bandaged hands and squirming bodies that fought with one another for the blanket to cover their nakedness.

Tossing and threshing back and forth, all the Rubens in the room felt themselves being ripped apart and bounced against ceiling, wall, shut door, floor, boarded-up window.

He was thinking that he was dying, when the door opened and Rebecca stood there, smiling, telling him it was time for supper.

V

When Crystal Gilbert came again, on Wednesday afternoon, he brought his girl Rosie along. She rode beside him in the pickup, braced against the door of the cab, her pigtailed hair bobbling up and down as Crystal took the ruts at top speed.

"Hello, Mason. Hello, Cousin Hilda," the sheriff said, piling out of his truck. "Good to see you again."

"Hello," Mr. Gilbert." Hilda stood on the front porch, her hands filled with dirt and flower seeds, a trowel sticking out of her apron pocket.

"Crystal," Mason greeted the sheriff with a smile, getting up from the porch steps where he was taking his rest.

"I wasn't expecting to see you again so soon," Crystal said with a big, stretch-mouthed smile, "but when I learned I had to come out to East Fork again, I brought Rosie along. Thought your girl Rebecca might enjoy a little friend to play with in the afternoons."

Hilda looked at Crystal gratefully. "Thank you so much, Mr. Gilbert," she said. "Rebecca is in her room. I'll call her." She took the young girl with her inside the white plank-board house.

"What brings you out our way again, Sheriff?" Mason Lawson asked, picking away idly at the burrs that were caught on his pants leg.

"Oh, rumors mostly," Crystal smiled. His big cheesey teeth shone from behind his thin-lipped grin. "Just rumors, Mason."

"Oh?"

"Yes, just rumors." The sheriff wasn't confiding.

"I see."

"You've been out in the fields, huh?" Crystal asked, looking at the burrs Mason was picking off. "It's been pretty weather for mending fences. I believe that's what you said you were doing."

"Yes, the boys and I've been working some this week. After school hours, of course."

"Of course."

There was a moment's silence between them. Then Crystal asked, "Did you ever get that barn cleaned out, Mason? Your boys were working on it last Saturday . . ."

"Oh, yes. They finished up that afternoon. Care to come and take a look at it?"

"Fine," Crystal said. The strain between them gave way, and they walked together out towards the barn.

Inside, Rebecca took Rosie Gilbert to her room and showed the girl her rag dolls.

"I've never seen a rag doll," Rosie said excitedly. "Where'd you buy this one? I like it."

"Buy it?" Rebecca asked. "Why, Mom made it for me. And my aunt made this one, the ballerina. My grandmom made this clown. It's bigger. She's going to show me how to make them soon, my grandmom is. She says I'm old enough to learn to make them for my little cousins."

"Oh, you've got cousins?"

"Dozens of them," Rebecca said proudly.

"They live up here?"

"No, up Fancy Creek, in the gap, and some of them clear over in MacPherson."

"My, my," Rosie shook her head, impressed.

"Haven't you got any?" Rebecca asked politely.

"No, not a single cousin. Not a brother or sister, either."

"I've got no sisters," Rebecca said. "But I do have three brothers."

"I've never seen any."

"No? They must be outside, playing."

"Do they go to school?"

"Bristol and Griffith do. Ruben doesn't. He's graduated from the eighth grade, though—that is, he was passed. He hasn't gone into high school yet. Pa's needed him around to help too much."

"Oh, I see."

The two girls fingered Rebecca's rag dolls some more. Rebecca let Rosie undress her dolls and feel the cotton stuffing that had been packed carefully inside them before they were hand stitched together and then dressed in clothes made from scraps of old shirts and dresses.

"They're so different from my dolls," Rosie said. "My dolls have foam rubber in them. Or they're plastic."

Rebecca looked puzzled.

"Plastic like in buckets," Rosie said.

Rebecca wondered how a hard plastic doll would feel to cuddle.

"If I come out again with Daddy, I'll bring one to show you," Rosie said. "I have lots of dolls, too. I don't really like them much, but Daddy says I'm too young to stop playing with them. He keeps bringing me more. Maybe I can give you one of them."

Rebecca's blue eyes shone eagerly. "I'd like to see one," she said timidly. "But I couldn't ask for one—"

Rosie grinned. "You'd not be asking," she said. "I have too many to keep up with. Besides, Daddy said I might offer you one."

"Oh," Rebecca frowned and wondered why Crystal Gilbert had said that. People in Passerman's Hollow didn't have so much that they could give it away right and left. But they didn't take handouts, either. Was the town so much different then? And the town people?

Rosie Gilbert didn't know she'd hurt Rebecca's feelings. Rosie was only nine, four years younger than Rebecca. She hummed to herself as she stroked the older girl's dolls, swaddling them in her arms and crooning lullabys she made up as she went along. Dolls were her babies, her brothers and sisters, her cousins. Her best friends. She told them everything and they listened. Even Rebecca's dolls listened. Rebecca must be as nice as her daddy said to have trained her dolls so well.

Rebecca, staring idly out the window, was aware of the little girl's plump arms, her brown pigtails, her freckled cheeks and smiling mouth. She was too young to really be friends with a thirteen-year-old girl. Then why did she come along with her daddy, Rebecca wondered?

Through the thin partitioned wall of her room, she could suddenly hear Ruben stirring around in his bed. With a start she wondered if Rosie realized that someone was in the room next to them, someone who was listening to their conversation and following their movements with his mind's eye.

"Rosie," Rebecca said at once, turning to the little girl with a smile, "Rosie, how would you like to take one of my dolls home to play with?"

"Really?" Rosie touched all the dolls spread out on Rebecca's bed. "Could I really? Are you sure?"

"Of course."

"Your mom wouldn't mind?"

"No."

"Not for keeps, though?"

"Well . . . you could bring it back the next time your daddy brings you out."

"All right. When I bring you one of mine?"

"That's right. We'll trade dolls for awhile."

"I'd like that. You won't miss yours, though?"

"No," Rebecca said. "I have enough to do. I have lots of homework, you know."

"What grade are you in?"

"Eighth next year," Rebecca said.

"Gee."

Rosie chose a pale-pink sailor doll dressed in white pants and shirt with a blue necktie and duffel bag thrown over his shoulder. "Could I take this one?"

"If you like."

Rosie clutched the doll close to her. "Thank you,

Rebecca," she said. "I'll call him Willie and I'll take care of him. He won't be lonely or get homesick."

They heard the motor of the blue pickup starting up.

"I guess that means I'd better go," Rosie said. "I enjoyed being with you, Rebecca." Her plump, round, short little legs took her to the door.

Rebecca watched her curiously.

"Oh," the girl turned around. "I'd like to come back and see you. You must be lonely now, not having a playmate and all."

"Yes," Rebecca said, "I get lonely."

At dinner, Ruben and Griffith and Bristol were discussing marbles.

"Blue ones roll best," Ruben said. "They're surer. They hit the reds ones, too. It's the red ones that's hard to knock out of the ring."

His two younger brothers looked up at him with much respect. Ruben was an eighth-grade graduate after all. He would be going on to high school soon, they assumed, after he'd finished helping Pa. He had won many marble tournaments in his time, too, so he must know what he was talking about.

"I guess you're right, Ruben," Bristol said. "Blue ones are the surest aim. Didn't you win against that Fritz boy shooting a blue one?"

"Yep. A surefire blue. With a dark streak down the center. Rolled that Fritz boy's red right off the ring. Beat out the best Fritz in the county." Ruben smiled.

Griffith and Bristol looked at each other. Then they said to Ruben, "We don't have a blue, Rube."

"Don't you really?"

"No. Every color but blue."

"Blue ones are hard to come by," Ruben said. "You got to work at collecting them. Sometimes it takes a lot of waiting to get a blue. But when you've got him, you're really ready to win."

"Huh? You got a blue, Rube?" Bristol asked.

"Yes. I've got two," Ruben said.

"Two?" the boys looked up.

"Why don't you give them to your brothers, Ruben?" Pa asked. "You don't shoot marbles anymore.

"No, but who knows?" Ruben said with a cagey smile. "Some morning I might wake up thinking this is the day I want to shoot marbles. And if I didn't have my Blue along, how'm I going to win?"

"I'd loan it back to you, Ruben," Bristol promised.

"So would I," Griffith said.

"Huh-uh. Loaning doesn't help," Ruben said. "It breaks the charm. You've got to own your Blue. You've got to keep him in your pocket, and warm him up now and again. You've got to feel him and roll him around between your fingers. You have to talk to him and reason with him and persuade him to win for you. You just can't trade a Blue back and forth and expect him to win."

"Oh." The boys' faces fell. They went back to forking their pie.

"But I'd consider trading you my Blue."

"A trade?" Griffith asked. "What've we got that you want, Ruben?"

"Sure," Bristol told his brother. "You name it and you're welcome to it."

"Hahahaha," Ruben laughed. "It's not that easy. I want something of Becky's."

"Becky's?" The boys looked at their mom and pa, puzzled.

"Yes. You've got to get Becky to give you something which you'll give to me."

"What is it, Ruben?" Rebecca asked.

Ruben shushed her with his finger over his lips. "I can't tell you, little sister," he said. "I have to tell these two—" and he reached for his brothers, pulling them close to him with one strong grip of his arm. He whispered something that made the little boys go into gales of laughter. They jumped up and ran up the stairs towards Rebecca's room.

"What on earth did you say, Ruben?" Hilda Lawson asked. There was merriment in her eyes from seeing her son Ruben teasing the others and enjoying himself so. Could it really be her Ruben, making a joyful noise, laughing so?

"You'll see, Mom," he told her. "You'll see."

Minutes passed. Then the boys came in and looked at Ruben strangely. "No," they said. "No, it wasn't there."

"What is it?" Rebecca asked. "What are you looking for?"

"Do you think she lost it?" Bristol asked.

"Becky?" Griffith looked at his sister. "How could she lose it? She never touches it."

Rebecca stared at them fixedly. "What'd you send them for, Ruben?" she asked him.

Ruben began to laugh.

"Tell me what it was."

"What was it, Bristol?" Pa asked.

Bristol hung his head.

"I said, what was it?" The father's voice was cold and meant business.

"Her doll."

"Doll? Rebecca doesn't play with dolls anymore."

"But she keeps them out in her room," Ruben said. "All sorts of them, scattered around over her bed and books and things . . ."

"Which doll do you want, Ruben?" Hilda Lawson asked, looking at Ruben's face so near to tears. "I'll go get it for you."

Ruben smiled up at his mother. "I want Willie the sailor doll," he said.

Mrs. Lawson could not find the sailor doll. She looked in the chest of drawers, under the chest, in the closet, under the bed, even inside Rebecca's pillowcase—thinking that for some reason her daughter might have stuck it there, to hide it, if this were some sort of game they were playing. But the sailor doll was not in Rebecca's room. Feeling uncertain of herself, not understanding her own ill feeling or her son Ruben's desire for a doll which was no longer in the house, she returned to the kitchen.

"Rebecca," she said, "the doll Ruben wants is not in your room."

Rebecca, trembling and tearful, lifted her head to meet her mother's eyes. "I know, Mom."

"You know?"

"Yes. I loaned it out."

"You loaned it?"

"Yes."

"But who to, Rebecca?"

"To Rosie Gilbert."

There was a triangular moment of understanding. Rebecca, her mother, and her father avoided each other's eyes. Bristol and Griffith, seeing that Ruben would not let them have his Blue, had lost interest in the conversation and run off to play before being sent to bed. Only Ruben remained at the table, waiting to be taken to his room, enjoying the discomfort he had created.

"Rosie said her father told her she could offer me a doll," Rebecca said, trying to make her voice light. "She offered to bring it to me the next time she comes out to visit. But I thought she might like to take one of mine home with her now—to play with until she comes again."

"Why don't you take Ruben to bed?" Hilda Lawson asked her husband abruptly. "Rebecca and I must get on with the dishes. Tomorrow is a school day."

Before his father could get up, Ruben, with a laugh, bounded up the stairs and into his room, slamming the door behind him.

VI

Mason Lawson was tired that night. He stretched out his six foot four inches in the bed he and his big brothers had made when they were living at the Homeplace. He had inherited the bed because he had been the last of the five boys to leave home and take a wife. None of the other brothers had felt they had a right to the bed, it belonged to the Homeplace as long as there was a Lawson brother living there to fill it. But when Mason married they all agreed it should go with him and save the brothers from another bed building. Up to then, when each Lawson boy married his brothers had built him a big four poster for a wedding present. But by the time Mason married, slow as he was to go on and ask Hilda although he'd been courting her for so long, they were tired of bed building. So Mason got the original Homeplace bed and Hilda had to sleep in it beside him knowing all his brothers had slept there at one time or another and feeling kind of funny about it. Now Hilda lay lost in what seemed to her lengths and lengths of soft feathery stuffing, curled up and close to the edge on her side of the Homeplace bed. She lay breathing quietly, her eyes closed to pretend sleep. She had grown used to lying on the edge, pretending sleep so that Mason would not hold her. That way she could reach down and touch the wooden railing, assuring herself of something solid and firm in the eerie softness of her husband's bed.

Mason did not close his eyes, but stared upward. His eyes seemed to penetrate the solid ceiling, the shingled roof of the house, the buttermilk clouded sky. Mason looked up at God and talked to him earnestly about what was troubling him so.

"What am I going to do with my boy?" he asked. "I don't feel right about keeping him around here. I don't know why, I just don't. There's something strange afoot. I can feel it in the air. I can sense it in his face, and Rebecca's. Sometimes even Bristol and Griffith show it in their eyes. What am I going to do?"

He allowed himself one inkling of hope. Maybe God was going to say *What think ye of Christ? Whose son is he?*

But God said nothing, and Mason continued to search his mind for the reasoning that lay behind his intuition. "I haven't sinned, God," he said. "I may not be completely honest with you in what I'm doing, but I haven't sinned openly or purposefully. Whatever it is that's happened, I don't know. I can only guess, but no parent can begin to believe those awful things about his children until he's confronted with them as truth, face to face, and the child spits in his eye and says 'Yes, it's true. I done it.' I'm leveling with you, God. And the honest-honest is, I don't believe there's guilt here. A strange thing has happened, but I don't know what it is."

He thought of Hilda, lying at his side, and knew that he should reach out and touch her. But he couldn't bring himself to put a hand on his wife's warm body. He felt that she was keeping him from God, she and her mother instinct for protecting even though she sensed what she protected was evil. *What, my son?* Yet she was vigilant because it was her child, it had come from her body. *And what, the son of my womb?*

To Mason, this was wrong, this was sin. One who had done evil must be rooted out, must be made to pay for his wrong. Regardless of who he was, or of how his mother and father felt, he must pay. Because he had sinned against another human being, who was really his brother or sister, and sinned against the true father God. *And they shall bear the punishment of their iniquity.*

Mason wanted to tell Hilda how he felt. He wanted to explain to her about how God had spoken to him in the church that Friday night Carla Adkins had disappeared. "Hilda," he wanted to say, "I was praying at the altar. I had my head on the railing and my feet tucked up under me. My hands were reaching over, touching the bottom of the preacher's pulpit, and I felt like I could lift up that church if God said to, and carry it up to Him. I struggled, Hilda. I felt the spirit of the Lord coming over me. My knees gave way and sagged against the rail. The preacher saw what was coming over me. He got down on his knees and held to me. He said, 'Go ahead and cry, Brother. Cry it out, and let them all hear you. Let them know that one in their midst has been touched.'

"But I just couldn't talk. I couldn't say a word they could make out. I just mumbled in the preacher's ear. But he understood me. He raised his eyes to Heaven, and he said 'O, God, this man speaketh in tongues.' And I did, Hilda. I spoke in the language of God. It wasn't mixed-up jumble, wife. It was the true language of the Lord, the tongue of all men."

He knew that Hilda would eye him strangely, and search his face to see if he spoke the truth or if he'd exaggerated the feelings he'd had. Hilda, with her plain, unrouged face, swigged-back hair and long-sleeved dresses, was like a piece of pure steel, ramming its way through a man's brain and heart and soul, testing every inch of him to determine his truth and honesty. Hilda was a demanding woman when it came to God. She had raised up their children, His children, with patience and modesty, teaching them Right and Wrong, showing them the true way to righteousness, watching over the boys for early signs of sin and corruption, and guarding Rebecca's virginity of mind as closely as she did her body's pureness.

But Mason felt a reluctance to speak of these things to Hilda. He was afraid that she would twist his words some way, or change around their meaning to show him that the child that so worried him must be protected, and it was his duty as a father to look after him. That it was sin to do otherwise and would endanger his dreams of salvation. For how could a man be saved if he denied his own and did not give them the strength and love they needed? For how could a child learn right from wrong, strength from weakness, love from hate if his own father would not show him the way? And how could that father hope for heaven when he had denied his children their most basic right, the right to God?

"But I'm a true man," Mason told himself. "A believer and a saved man. I live by the laws of God, and Heaven will be my reward. The sweet heaven paved with streets of gold, the heaven where choirs of angels are perched up in the clouds and winged chariots of silver carry the prophets to speak to us multitudes of simple men. I'm a saved man and I will sip the honeyed wine and break the manna of God with my fellow men, all of us saved, hallelujah, sitting there in Heaven at the feet of our Lord and joining in the choirs of angels. Amazing Grace. This is my dream. And nothing will keep my dream from coming true. I'll not sin against God—I'll not break His laws or endanger my chances with the Holy Ghost. I'll do what I must do, I'll do what I know is right. This life is just a trial. It's a trial to see if I'm fit for the next. I must be strong. I must be ready."

Hilda, her long hair woven up in the night's braids, wrapped her flannel gown around her for warmth and lay there quietly, trying to decipher the thoughts that were crossing her husband's mind.

"It's Ruben," she figured. "He's worried about Ruben. He's scared. He doesn't understand what's happened, and he's afraid that things will get worse. He doesn't know what's made the boy the way he is—he thinks he's sinned and this is his punishment."

"Well, maybe it is," her firm mouth knotted in hard lines. "Maybe it is his punishment for thinking he was so almighty. If he'd not been so selfish, if he'd have thought more of his family, of the three boys, his girl, and his wife, then he'd not have an idiot boy locked in his room upstairs."

Hilda grimaced and longed to leave this man's big bed and go take Ruben in her arms and nurse away his fever. "Mason Lawson," she thought, "if you'd have been more concerned about just living out this life as a God-fearing man instead of toying about with the ideas of eternal happiness and reward for your goodness, if you'd of been content with earthly happiness before you reached the eternal, maybe you'd have already found some recompense. Maybe you'd of made a decent happy home where we could praise the Lord by reaping the fruits of the rich harvest His love has sown. As it is, you've only created despair when you've lifted your hands and devoted yourself to the eternal.

"I know you, Mason," Hilda mumbled into the sheet. "I know you well. You and your *Blessed are ye that weep now, for ye shall laugh.* Better to laugh a little now and take your chances on weeping later. Better to laugh a little now with your wife and family and keep your eye on this kingdom of God, instead of your heart set on the next. The Lord worketh in many ways, and he didn't make this world just to be squandered away on dreams of the next."

And then, remembering Mason's exhibitionism at Friday-night church, Hilda frowned disgustedly. "I saw you, Mason," she thought. "I saw you throwing yourself into the arms of the preacher, thinking he was God come to give you your salvation just when you wanted it. I know you, Mason. I saw you roll your eyes and jarble your tongue about in your mouth. I saw you hug the preacher and away as if you was about to swoon. And I saw you get up with your pants soaked."

Being a woman and able to control all her emotions without showing pleasure or pain unless she wanted, Hilda felt contempt for men who were forever panting about as if they would die if they did not get what they were after.

"You're a real sinner, Mason," she said to herself. "You're a man of so much selfishness and sin that you're unable to rear your family properly. I saw that a long time ago. I've been looking after us since before the first one was born. And I'm taking care to weed out seeds of the father before they can be planted in another. You'll not teach your sons to do the things you do, or share your hopeless dreams. I'll see to that.

"But," Hilda realized, "I must do something now."

She thought of Mason's quietness, his stealthy thoughts, his limp, energyless body. "He's planning something," she decided. "He's planning something to do to Ruben. He wants Ruben away, before he can spoil the relationship Mason has with God. Mason is afraid of God—he's afraid to stick up for the boy, because God might say it's wrong. Mason doesn't believe that God might try him, to see if he's willing to sacrifice for the boy. He thinks he must be Jacob, and give this son the knife—he'll gladly let the boy go if it will ensure his own safety, his salvation, his own private hallelujah. But I'll do the bargaining, not you, Mason." Hilda smiled. She knew God was a man, therefore he could be taken by women who were his superior. A man feared his own sex; but a woman, an intelligent woman, could work God easier than she could her own husband.

"I'll beat him at his own game," Hilda thought of Mason and tweaked the corners of her mouth in an ironic smile. "If he wants Ruben to go away, he can go. But I'll be the one to send him away. I'll send for Colby Chaser in the morning."

❋   ❋   ❋

Hunky Miller's face peering through the windowpane told Hilda that her stepfather was on his way up. She set the coffee on the stove to warm and measured out the flour, baking powder, salt for biscuits. She went to the cellar for fresh preserves while the stove was heating.

Mason was out. That was good. He had eaten breakfast and gone off before the children went to meet the bus. After putting Ruben back in his room, Hilda had gone to change her dress and do up her hair freshly. Colby Chaser liked to see her nice looking.

The old man came in, kicking off his muddy boots, propping his cane noisily against the wall, knocking his cap down on the table. He took out a dirty handkerchief and blew his nose into it. His white hair glistened with morning wind and sweat drops, his ruddy cheeks were flushed bright pink from the climb up the hill to Hilda's house.

"I left right after you called," he said to Hilda, bending down to kiss her cheek. "That hill of yours keeps getting steeper."

Hilda smiled and laughed at the same time. "I guess it does, stepdaddy," she said. "Every winter scrapes some off its slopes."

Colby Chaser unbuttoned his navy blue pea jacket and showed the bright plaid flannel shirt he was wearing underneath. He took the chair Hilda offered him and sipped on the coffee she poured out, watching her as she patted milk on the biscuits and slid them in the oven.

"I figured you needed me," Colby said as he began his second cup.

"Yes," Hilda set down a new pat of butter and a clear dish of preserves. "Yes, stepdaddy, I need you. I've got a favor to ask of you."

"Ask away."

"It's one of my boys. He's turned sickly."

Colby Chaser's startling white hair seemed to mellow into a kind, snowy-cropped color and his blue eyes flickered gently as he took Hilda's bony, knuckled hand in his own and said, "I'm sorry to hear that."

"Yes," Hilda said, turning her face away.

"Which is it?"

"Ruben, your favorite."

"Oh." The old man shook his head and stared at the floor. Ruben. "What does Mason know of it?" he asked at last.

"Mason knows he's sick," Hilda said quickly. "He doesn't know what ails him."

"Do you?"

"No," Hilda said. "No, stepdaddy, I don't. But he's a sick boy, and it's getting hard to keep him here around the well ones."

"I see."

"Can you take him for a while?" Hilda asked at last, turning her face toward the table where Colby Chaser sat over his coffee. "Can you keep him on the farm and look after him until I think things are—steady enough—for me to send for him?"

"You know I can."

Hilda's strained unnatural expression relaxed. Tiny tears bubbled up in the corners of her eyes, tinting the pure blue into a thick opaqueness. Colby Chaser smiled admiringly. "I'll do anything I can to help," he said. "Anything."

"Thank you." Hilda dried her tears on the cuffs of her dress sleeves.

"When do you want him to go?" Colby asked.

"Now," Hilda said.

"Before his daddy comes in for lunch?"

"Yes. That might be better. Can you manage him?"

"Will he get along with Hunky?"

"Yes, stepdaddy. He and Hunky play fine together."

"Then why don't you call your brother and explain to him?" Colby asked.

"All right." Hilda got up.

"Tell me, girl," Colby said, his clever eyes following her unsteadiness. "Is it Miller sickness?"

"I don't know," Hilda looked at her stepfather and answered honestly. "I just don't know. I don't think so, but I can't be sure."

Colby nodded, and watched his stepdaughter go out to find Hunky. Where would Hunky be? Probably squatting down under a pine tree, playing with the cones he could pry from the mud with a stick. Or maybe rolling in a fresh patch of greening grass, crooning himself a song, pretending he was the wind.

The woman, finding him, stooped down by the flower

bushes and put her hands on the thirty-year-old man's shoulders.

"Hunky," she said.

"Hi, hi," her brother grinned.

"Hi, yourself. Hunky, I've got news for you."

"Good news?"

"Good news."

"The moon has a baby, and now there'll be two for Hunky to play with?"

"No."

"The world will turn to angel cake in spring and the sun will be lemonade spilling over it?"

"No."

"Somebody's coming to stay with me?"

"Yes," Hilda said. "Do you know who?"

"Ruben," he said simply.

"That's right. How did you know?"

Gesturing with the back of his hand, Hunky motioned to Ruben's room on the second floor of the white plank house. Two of the boards had been removed from the window, and the boy was standing there, grinning and waving down at Hunky. When Ruben saw his mother watching, he reached through the open space with the board he had taken down, and patched up the hole.

"Are you glad to have Ruben as a playmate?"

"Yes."

"Will you be good to him?"

"Yes."

"Will you look after him?"

"Yes."

While he was waiting for his stepdaughter to come back, Colby Chaser walked restlessly through the house, going from room to room, scrutinizing the plain polished furniture, the lack of clutter in its arrangement, the spotless cleanliness of the floors and walls and windows. He noticed a ball of bright red wool in Hilda's round sewing basket, on top of the socks she was darning, and wondered who could be making something so bright and pretty.

"It must be Rebecca," he thought. "She'd be liking a bright color like that, with her blue eyes and yellow hair."

Then he became aware through the rising bumps on his arms that someone was standing at the top of the stairs, looking down at him. Softly, he turned and called out, "Ruben?" but the pitter-patter of naked feet and a muffled giggle were his only answer.

"I wonder how long they've had the boy shut up," he asked himself. "A week or two? Or more? It must have taken Hilda some talking to get Mason to allow it. Mason's probably scared to death, ready to send the child off or turn him over to whoever wants him." And Colby shuddered at the thoughts of Hilda's sick child being abandoned.

"She knew to send for me, though," he smiled. "She knew I'd understand. I understood about it when I married her mother. Hunky was sicker then than he is now. Sick, but harmless. Not violent, the way Mona was. No, not like Mona. Suspicious she was, and mean and sneaky to the very end, harboring evil thoughts and ideas against me—hating her own daughter, too, because of all those sick nagging suspicions she wouldn't let her own powers of reason explain."

Colby didn't like to think about Mona Miller. He didn't like to have to remember her the way she really was. He liked to think of her occasionally, when he passed a tree she had liked, or saw a sunset she would have thought beautiful. When he opened up his tin of tobacco and knew how she would have grumbled at his spilling shreds of it out on the floor, grumbled and then smiled as she cleaned it up and told him that it was his home, he could do as he liked there, she loved him and only wanted to be good to him and show him a wife's respect. He didn't like to remember Mona sulking and vicious, hating him, hating Hilda, loving only her sick son Hunky because she was afraid that no one else would. Miller sickness. But at least he had known how to handle it.

"I hate to see it come to Hilda's family," Colby said to himself. "A man like Mason doesn't know how to cope with these things. Mason can use his hands to build bars to keep the boy in, but he can't use his mind to make the boy well. And Hilda can't fight it alone, with three others to look after."

Once again, laughter at the top of the stairs.

"Ruben?" Colby called a little louder.

The sounds of a footstep.

"Ruben?"

Another step. Then more laughter, pitter-patter, the slam of a door, and the boy was back in his room.

Hilda came in through the kitchen door, with an armful of freshly ironed clothes she had picked up from the pantry.

"These are the boy's," she said. "I'll put them in a box."

"Hunky knows?" Colby asked.

"He knew all along," Hilda said. "Ruben was signaling him from the window. There won't be any trouble."

"Do you think he'll tire on the way?"

"He'll run you down getting there. He's tired of being all cooped up."

Colby nodded, watching Hilda make up the box, adding cookies and gingerbread and apples in its corners.

"Tell Ruben to give some to Hunky," she said.

A scraping on the ceiling told them both that Ruben knew to share with his idiot uncle.

"Where's Mason working today?" Colby asked casually.

"South meadow. Mending fences."

"Then we'll take the north meadow, by Passerman's Hollow. We'll be home in a couple of hours."

"Fine." Her mouth trembled.

"That's not too far away, Hilda. The boy can come

back when he wants to. Don't think you're losing him."

"I know."

"And I'll look after him as well as I can. You can trust me."

Hilda was silent. Then she said, "You'd better go now. Mason will be in soon. It's close to dinnertime."

"Greens?" Colby asked, pressing his nose against the big blue pan on the rear burner of the cook stove.

"Greens," Hilda grinned, herself again.

"You needn't ask me to stay for lunch, girl," Colby said. He smiled and patted her cheek. "Another time."

"Ruben," Hilda said, knocking on the boy's door. "Ruben?"

There was no answer.

"Ruben, I'm coming in."

She turned the key in the lock and entered the boy's room. Her stepfather followed her.

"He's gone," she said.

The boarding-up planks were stacked neatly on the floor, beneath an open window. The nails that Ruben had pried out with his fingers were arranged in an orderly row, from the largest to the smallest, on the top board. Through the gaping window hole, Hilda and Colby Chaser could see Ruben and Hunky, racing each other through the mud-sloppy tender shoots of greenness, down the hill and over the pasture towards the north meadow.

VII

Mason, who had not come in for lunch at all, ate hungrily at the supper table. It was a quiet meal. Rebecca sat with downcast eyes, staring thoughtfully at her brother Ruben's empty place. Bristol and Griffith, who were never noisy, scraped at their plates without enthusiasm and seemed lost in their own thoughts, far away from sharing any their family might have.

Mason had prayed grace quickly, making none of the fervent overtones he usually made to God when he asked for the evening meal and the hands who prepared it to be blessed. This time Mason only bowed his head, mumbled beneath his breath, then asked for bread.

Hilda, stern and upright in her ladder-back chair, her eyes even with those of her husband and children, said nothing to encourage or discourage the conversation. She only waited.

In their room that evening, after supper was done, the kitchen cleaned and the children gone to their beds, Mason said to his wife, "I saw Colby Chaser walking off towards the north meadow at noon."

"Did you?" Hilda asked, brushing her long hair and getting ready to wind it into braids.

"That's why I didn't come in."

"I missed you at noon. There was no one here but myself. It was lonely."

"Did you send Ruben with him?"

"Ruben wanted to go."

"Your brother Hunky was along?"

"Yes."

Mason shook his head. He stretched out a hand, imploringly, and reached for his wife's almost bare back. Startled, Hilda pulled her gown tighter to hide her unwilling nakedness.

"Hilda, wife," Mason said. "Do you think that was best?"

"What else was there to do?" the woman said. "You've told me you wanted the boy away. You've prayed for him to go. I saw no place else to send him. Besides, what harm is Hunky? And stepdaddy will look after . . ."

"Hunky is no harm," Mason said quickly. "But he can't help Ruben. He can't make him stronger. It's just a way of encouraging the boy's strange-mindedness."

And you, Mason, she wanted to say. What did you do to help him? What have you ever done for any of us who was weak? But she only asked, "And Colby? What's wrong with Colby?"

"Colby is an old man. A strange old man. And I don't trust him," Mason said bluntly.

Hilda drew up in the big bed where she was sitting, winding her braids, and pulled the ironed sheets up even with her chin to hide her heaving chest. She was hurt and mad that Mason was going to bring up her family and throw their queerness in her face.

"There's no reason not to trust stepdaddy," she hissed at him finally, unable to hold her temper back any longer. She hated to argue family, but after all, she thought, someone had to defend them. And Colby—good old Colby with his hunting guns and bright blue eyes so quick to spot a rabbit or a lie or someone holding something from before against him. Good old Colby might be an old man— even a strange old man—with messy habits, but he was God-fearing and he took care of his own. "You've got no reason not to trust him," she said, shaking her head.

"Oh, no?" Mason couldn't believe his wife's words. "Your own mom died married to him. And she died a strange way."

"She choked to death."

"Says Colby."

"Mason," Hilda lowered her trembling voice, "Mason, if you're trying to say something . . ."

"I'm not trying to say anything, Hilda. I just worry about the boy living in that strange house."

"He's more welcome there than you made him here," Hilda snapped.

Mason shrugged his big shoulders angrily and reached for his wife. "Now, listen," he said. "You know why I felt that way. I was afraid for the others. I just had a bad feeling. Well, maybe I was wrong. Maybe I got off on the wrong track. Look how quiet Bristol and Griffith were tonight. Look how unhappy little Becky was . . ."

"A few days ago you said Rebecca was almost a grown woman. You said we should look out for her more. I'm trying to do it now."

"Maybe it's the wrong way."

"It's the way you suggested; it's what you wanted."

"But she loves Ruben."

"She has Griffith and Bristol to play with. She has you and me."

Mason said, "But there was something special between her and Ruben. They understood each other. Rebecca could control him."

"Maybe it was Ruben controlling her," Hilda said, turning her moody eyes to the wall and pulling away from Mason's grip.

His heart hammering from the arguing, his brain mad over the way his wife had twisted his intentions to suit her own means, Mason pulled up and faced the other wall. "I don't want to quarrel all night," he said. "I need my sleep. I've got to work tomorrow. But I do want to say this, wife. I don't approve of your sending away one of my children without at least telling me about it."

"I didn't send him away," Hilda said. "I told you he wanted to go. And you wanted him to. There wasn't any place else to send him. And there wasn't any place else I'd want him to go. You've never been able to make up your mind about anything. So don't come barking after me when I do it for you."

Angrily, Mason Lawson threw down the covers and edged toward his wife.

*　　*　　*

Running barefoot in the wind, Ruben carried his shirt and jeans in one hand and waved his other as if to sweep back wave-currents of watery air that slapped at his naked body. Over the hills he came, his hair stringing down his neck, rain plastered to his wetted skin. His eyes stayed open wide, bright blue thunder bolts glaring out as he whizzed his way over mud, leaping over ditches, skimming over logs, slashing his way through piles of dead, clogged-up leaves. The white plank house on the hill was in sight, and Ruben crunched behind the stile at the meadow fence to look at it. In the rainy blackness, he could barely make out its edges. If there had been no light in Rebecca's room, he would not have been able to see his way up.

Running on, he twirled his body madly, jumping and leaping, swirling in the wind, splashing in the mud, wiping his rainy hands against his warm, damp thighs. The night was beautiful, it was black and hideous, a cramped-up blind ghost that no violet eyes could see through. Pausing only to let the rain wash him off and then to dress quickly, Ruben grabbed the loose planks he knew well and slithered himself up the back side of the house, stepping on window frames, clinging to shingles and bent boards. His body, lithe, muscular, controlled, made no noise; his hands, clinging like claws to their holds, never slipped. He swung himself through his window and collapsed, panting happily, on his rollaway. Snuggling down beneath the blanket, he rolled his head from side to side on the pillow, drying his hair.

Then he grew lonely.

It was lonely lying there in that room.

Careful to let no board creak, he slipped out the door, down the hall, and rapped on Rebecca's door.

"Yes?" the girl whispered.

Ruben pushed the door open with his fingertips and

slipped across the threshold. He stood inside Becky's room, smiling shyly, waiting for praise.

Rebecca, sitting cross-legged in her bed, reading absentmindedly from a literature book, showed no surprise at seeing her brother there although her heart was pounding.

She smiled at him.

"You knew I'd come?" Ruben asked, nervously, rubbing his hands together.

Rebecca nodded.

He came closer, until he could stand on her hand crocheted rug and warm his bare feet.

"How was it tonight?" he asked.

"Awful."

"Did they quarrel?"

"Not till they went to bed."

"Have they gone to sleep?"

"I don't think so."

"Are they still talking?"

"They're whispering."

"Let's go see," Ruben said impetuously.

"We can't, Ruben."

"Of course we can." The boy's chin jutted up, his bright blue eyes shot fire. "Come on. I'll help you."

"But Ruben, we can't! The boards will creak—and their door is locked. There's no way to peek in, when they've got the key in the keyhole."

"There's a window."

"No!" Rebecca's face showed horror and fright and fascination mingled with her curiosity and her desire to spend as much time as she could with her brother. But to do this! What he was suggesting was . . .

"Yes!" Ruben knew that he was winning and he pressed on. "Come on! You'll have to tie up your gown, it might catch on the nails. And put on a scarf to hide your hair. It's raining."

"Oh, no, Ruben."

"Not very hard, though. You won't really get wet. I won't let you."

"Oh, Ruben."

Her heart pounding, her whole body throbbing, Rebecca slid from the bed and stood with bare feet on the edge of the crocheted rug. She took a dress sash from her closet and hooked it around the waist of her long gown, pulling it up several inches from the floor. Then she covered her hair with a heavy scarf. Ruben watched her, grinning, excitement thumping in his chest. He was having an adventure, an adventure with Becky!

When she was ready, he took her hand in his and led her to the door of her bedroom. He cracked his head into the hall to make sure that it was empty even though he knew it would be. No one in the house would be stirring this late. Except him. Then he led his sister very carefully into his room, showing her how to walk so that she stepped on the balls of her feet with her toes spread out and made no noise. They crossed the floor of his room, Ruben zigzagging and Becky following, careful to avoid the creaking boards that Ruben pointed out to her. Then he reached the open window and swung himself through the frame, setting his feet down firm on the roof of the kitchen stoop. It was only a small jump, it would give Becky no trouble. He reached up for his sister's hands.

She gave them to him willingly. He pulled her out slowly, positioned her feet in the wind, signaled her to drop and helped her gain her balance on the roof. When she had stopped shivering from fear mingled with the sudden chill of rain soaking her and the cool wind blowing through her dampness, Ruben scrambled up across the roof, clinging to the kitchen chimney. This time Rebecca did not wait for him to reach for her. She followed eagerly, carefully, mimicking his supple movements, her body crawling rhythmically and quietly along the rough, jagged surface of the rooftop.

On they went, on, on through the night, across the sky,

behind the moon, into the valley of the stars where lost kings slept and dreamed of winter castles covered with clean white snow, their queens beside them remembering spring and flower tapestries that hung against cold castle walls. On past desert wells fulls of pure blue water where they stopped to drink, on across mountains of cold sand and black bone trees. On and on while the rain fiddled a dance tune and their feet tapped time as they flew through the magic air.

When they came to the top of the world, the peak of the roof, Ruben signaled for Rebecca to wait. He went over first, digging his fingers in for holds, groping with his feet for a firm place to catch in. He lay for a moment, stretched on the rack. Then he dropped, sliding down to the front-porch roof with a gentle, even thud.

He reached up for Rebecca. She shivered, squatting on her haunches and peeking over. Her gown was drawn up farther, pulled tight to keep her warm, and through the gray blackness of the night Ruben could scarcely make out the features on her excited face. Only the curve of her lips, the gleam in her eye, made him see that she was ready. He lifted up his hand and beckoned to her.

Suffer the little children to come unto me.

As she had seen him do, Rebecca turned herself around and stretched out flat on the roof. Her fingers found Ruben's holds in the shingles. But her feet stuck. She could not release herself. Squirming her body up and down, she forced her stuck gown to slide down beneath her legs until it was even with her feet. Then she could move. She let go. She slid.

Ruben, waiting, stopped her with his shoulders and helped pull her up from the little hump she had crumbled into. She was breathing heavily. He put his hand across her mouth to stop the swift intake of air. He felt her mouth twitch in relief, then curl into a smile. Their eyes met, glittering with excitement. For a moment, they faced each other, triumphant in the first part of their little adventure, each resting a moment before the climax. Then Ruben nodded that it was time to go on. He went first, stepping lightly, his hands flailing the wind as if to suspend the most of his weight in the air.

Rebecca followed. They glided across the roof and crouched, near its edge, listening for sounds to come up from their parent's bedroom.

Down inside they heard only a low, sharp moan, followed by the sounds of Hilda Lawson moving abruptly, the rustle of covers being jerked about her, her breath whispering, "No!"

Ruben flattened himself out and rolled over until he could see in through the bedroom window. He pulled Rebecca with him. Although they were hidden by the darkness, they were so close to their mother that they held their breaths and kept their faces flat on the roof, their eyes turned in from the rain, their hair wet and crawling on their necks, both of them terrified that Hilda could hear or see them they were so close to the window.

Hilda was sitting on the edge of the bed, shaking, her face contorted with tears. "Leave me alone," she said.

Then they saw their father's huge bulky body jolt upwards and his long arms shoot out towards his wife. He looked like a snake making its strike.

"No," Hilda hissed again. "Leave me alone."

Mason said nothing. But his mouth was set and this time he took the gown in his hands and ripped it from his wife's neck to her stomach, reaching inside for her breasts as soon as it had cleaved open.

Horrified, Hilda tried to pull back. "Stop it," she whispered. "Stop it, please, Mason." She stumbled out of bed and began to edge backwards towards the window.

The children, pressed down against the roof, their bodies touching for warmth in the cool night wind, could see only disgust and fear on their mother's face before she turned her back to them. But their father's face was lit up with the mean glow in his eyes and a thin stream of silvery saliva leaked out of the left-hand corner of his mouth as he followed his wife out of their bed, stalking her to the window where she could go no farther. He stood there for a long moment, stark naked, listening to his wife's tears. Then he pulled the long muslin gown, the kind Rebecca was wearing, down over Hilda's cringing body and threw it on the floor.

Rebecca lay with her eyes shut, sobbing quietly to herself, but she knew Ruben was watching. She could feel the tenseness going in and out of his body and she knew he wanted to pull away from her but there was no place he could go. She lay there in the rain, crying quietly to herself, until Ruben touched her hand and said, "It's all right, Becky, we can go now."

VIII

Rebecca was sick and could not go to school. Her mother noticed the flush in the child's cheeks, and an unusual, thick, glazed brightness in her eyes. When she began to sneeze, Hilda sent her upstairs to bed with a cup of camomile tea.

Rebecca, wincing from the touch of her mother's hand, went unwillingly. She wanted to go to school. She did not want to miss class. She did not want to stay at home. But Hilda would not hear to it, and Mason said she must stay in bed.

When she had cleared their breakfast dishes and strained the morning's milk, Hilda made milk toast and took it upstairs to her daughter.

She found her lying in bed, looking out the window.

"Rebecca," Hilda stood there, the bowl of frothing, sugared, milk-sopped bread in her hand. "Rebecca, I've brought you something good."

"I'm not hungry."

"But you must eat. You'll grow weak."

Rebecca turned over on her stomach and buried her face in the pillow. "I'm not hungry," she repeated.

Hilda set the dish down carefully on Rebecca's dresser scarf and left the room.

For a week Rebecca lay in bed, her eyes burning with fever. She grew faint from hunger, sick and empty in the pit of her stomach, but she would not touch anything brought to her by her father or mother. She ate only what Griffith or Bristol carried up from the supper table, or what Ruben smuggled in to her in his pockets—crumbling bread, a candy bar, an apple, a piece of cake. She lay in bed, flat on her stomach mostly, her head turned to the window, not doing a thing. She showed no interest in her schoolwork, and fell behind although her teacher sent assignments home by her brothers. She would not read or do her arithmetic. She lay in bed on her stomach, looking out the window or closing her eyes to the room around her.

Rosie Gilbert came again, with her father Crystal, and was allowed to go up to the sick girl's room. ("Maybe she can cheer Becky up," Hilda Lawson told the sheriff. "I just don't know what to do for her. I don't have an idea left in my head.") Rosie returned the sailor doll Willie, whom she had nicknamed Tie-Tie because of his bright blue tie, and offered to lend Rebecca a store-bought doll of her own. Rebecca snatched back her sailor doll eagerly and tucked it under her pillow. But she would have nothing to do with Rosie's doll. The pink nylon dress, the frizzy, yellow, wash-and-set hair, the open-and-shut eyes with even brown lashes, the blank face of the doll staring at her made Rebecca put her head in her hands and dive beneath the covers, frightening Rosie.

The little girl ran out to her father and said she wanted to go home. Alarmed, Hilda hurried to Rebecca's room and found her daughter weeping over the sailor doll. Puzzled, Hilda said nothing, but went slowly back downstairs to say good-by to the sheriff. ("She just got tired. She's awful weak yet.")

The next day, when she came up to change Rebecca's sheets and dust the room, the sailor doll had disappeared.

Rebecca watched for signs of spring through her window. She saw sprouts of fragile green grass pushing their way up through taut brown earth; she watched them wiggle in the wind, bending their tips in belly laughter when fuzzy fingered breezes tickled their middles. The sun was a hot coral circle singeing the blue sky as it sucked up the earth's moistness and dragged out what life had been mellowing beneath its wintery surface.

Ruben, when he came to visit in the early morning hours of each day's dawn, told her of his prowls through the hills and the spring things he had discovered. Crouching on the floor, viewing her from the distance of the room, Ruben would draw earth pictures with his arms and fill them in delicately by rubbing his fingers across their aerial surface, coloring, tinting, etching, as he squeezed and pricked the pastel air.

"Flowers bigger than trees," Ruben would say, "with big yellow bodies that bounce and flounce in the wind. The grass is high, Becky. It'll never be mowed this summer. It's giant's grass. North meadow is already green as ice, fragrant with the scent of a sweet secret."

Rebecca would listen on.

"And the hills! You should run down them! Little sister, all you do is stand on top. And your feet start to slide! They carry you down, down, down the slicky slide into a nest of milkweed's pod and warm soft moss.

"The morning sky, it's a carnival of blues and violets and pinks. You ought to watch right before the sun comes out. The sky goes wild, it explodes with color—whoom!" And Ruben would clash his hands together, never making a noise but sending vibrations of the tremendous explosion across the room to his sister.

When Hunky Miller, who came with him many times, whistled from behind a rosebush, Ruben knew it was time to leave. He would slip from the room without a word of good-by, finishing his story with gestures. Once he crossed the bare boards, skirting the hand-crocheted rug, and touched his sister's forehead with the back of his hand. The heat of her fever frightened him, and he jumped back instinctively.

❖   ❖   ❖

After a week of lying in bed, Rebecca sat up on Saturday morning, pushed her feet into her red-felt bedroom slippers, pulled on a robe and went downstairs to help with breakfast.

Her mother was surprised, but said nothing. She saw that the flush was gone from her daughter's face, and her eyes were calm. Rebecca went about her usual chores, but more slowly than usual because of her weakness. She cooked the cereal and strained the milk and smiled when her father and brothers came in and sat down at the oil-cloth-covered table.

The boys seemed eager to cheer Rebecca and during the meal they tried to include her in their Saturday plans.

"Mom and Pa are going to town, Becky," Bristol said, "but we're going to stay at home. You want to go or stay?"

"Stay," Rebecca said.

And I will let you go, and ye shall stay no longer.

"You want to come play with us?" Griffith asked.

"Pa says we can play while he's gone, if we do up the chores now. You want to play with us?" Bristol smiled, shaking his golden hair and dreaming of a green spring world that lay beyond the kitchen windows.

Rebecca nodded, toying with her spoon.

"We're going outside. We're going to shoot marbles."

"I can't shoot," Rebecca said.

"Yes, you can," Griffith told her.

"You can even win," Bristol added.

"How?"

"I'll let you have my Blue," Griffith said.

"Or mine." Bristol began fishing for his marble in his pocket. "See?" He held up his round, blue, glass ball.

Rebecca smiled wanly.

Hilda was sick after breakfast. She went to the bathroom and stayed for fifteen minutes. Rebecca heard her retching, and she flushed the commode twice. The girl smiled to herself as she cleared off the table and stacked the dishes.

When her mother reappeared, her face was pale and gray. Her eyes were dull, lusterless, and her face twitched from the motions of being sick. She sank down at the table and put her head in her hands. "How can a seed grow that quickly?" she asked herself. "Or is it just me afraid? Or maybe it was planted sometime before? Why can't I know when it was that life started. It might make a difference how I was to feel about it." Hilda shut her eyes and let the blackness help quiet her stomach and hurting throat.

"Here, Mom." Rebecca brought her mother hard bread and fresh strong tea.

Hilda took it slowly and began to chew on the edge of the bread as she sipped the warm tea from the freshly rinsed cup.

"This tastes good," she said at last. "How'd you know this is what I needed?"

"It's what you always asked for the last time," Rebecca said.

They wrapped up Rebecca in a warm wool sweater and jeans beneath her cotton dress because the wind was sharp and the sun still too weak to spare them much heat.

Bristol and Griffith were like moles, burrowing their way through meadow grass, creeping through thinly ridged, sharp barbed-wire fence instead of going over the stile or through the gate, leaping creek banks, swinging on grapevines.

"Dare you!" Griffith would scream, jerking his head in the direction of a loose hanging branch.

Glaring back defiantly, Bristol would seize the branch and swing himself clumsily to and fro, holding his feet up off the ground, bending over double and gritting his teeth with effort. There he would go like a great golden-feathered bird sailing through the morning air, an eagle or a dove or a sparrow shimmering in the pale green air.

Then, dropping to soft earth that gave way beneath his plopped-down weight and made him struggle briefly for balance, he would throw the branch back at his brother and wait for him to take his turn.

Wiry Griffith beat him easily, shinnying up the rough grapevine, clawing at it with one hand while with the other he groped for other branches to pull himself on to.

He could climb a whole tree this way, beating his way up on pure air and an overhanging branch.

Rebecca and Bristol would watch him, their hearts in their throats, their chests thumping fiercely with fright and sickening excitement that made them urge him on, higher, higher. Rebecca would never understand how such a little boy could go so high so fast and even Bristol envied him his speed and agility. But Griffith was little and wiry and strong, an earth child born and bred. And Bristol —everything that Bristol lacked in strength he made up for in the grace of his slender body and the dreamy glow of his clear blue eyes. Bristol was just a different breed of boy.

Rebecca walked with the wind in her face, her smooth long fingers gently caressing grass blades, poking beneath budding flowers, picking up and turning over smooth stones. Coming to a flat rock, she stretched out on her back and turned her face to the sun, soaking up what rays the winds did not carry on to needy grasses.

Here she hummed to herself as she toyed with the dark moss clumps clotted to the rock. She dug her slender feet in tighter against the flanks of her gritty bed, and pushed her nose down deep into the lichen, forcing herself to smell the rot fragrance of beat-out, worn-out life still clinging to its own.

"Ugh." She gagged and pressed her hands to her stomach, then her throat. The sweet, sickly smell permeated her flesh until she darted up and away after the two boys.

At the north meadow, Griffith and Bristol walked about thoughtfully, searching out a fine, flat piece of ground without rocks or lumps or damp spots. With a grunt, Bristol signaled that he had found the spot. He squatted down and drew a ring in the soft dirt. On each side of it, the boys knuckled up and dumped their marbles in the center.

Clink clink. The bright-chipped glass balls rolled out

of their little sock sacks and onto the pan-shaped ground. The color spots that made eyes on each marble seemed to glare fiercely about the ring, sizing up opponents and winking threats.

Squinting up at the sun Bristol aimed and shot at Griffith's cluster. He knocked out three. With a smile, he sank back on the grass and waited for his brother to take his turn.

Griffith hunched over the glass armies and plotted out his strategy. Then he rolled his Blue back and forth in his warm, sweaty little hand, caressing it, petting it, warming it. He aimed and shot. Five of Bristol's marbles rolled outside the ring.

"Uh."

"Oh."

The game went on, stopping only while the boys wiped off their foreheads or their sticky hands on a patch of towel-soft grass. Sometimes, one would comment to the other on how a shot could have been better made. Bristol, who was usually behind, would nod gratefully for his younger brother's advice.

They played four games, Griffith always winning. Then they sank back on their haunches and thought of nothing, letting their small, boyish bodies fade into the giant raw earthiness of the spring day.

From behind his head, where fishes were swimming in warm April creeks and new young birds were flying across the meadow grass, Bristol saw Rebecca standing back, one foot behind the other, watching shyly.

"Come on, Becky," he called. "Take on the champ."

"Sure," Griffith yelled. "I'll play you."

"I'll help you," Bristol promised, as an eagle soared across his thoughts.

"He's pretty good," Griffith said. "The two of you might beat me."

"Come on, Becky."

She drew near, coming sideways as if she were being swept along cautiously by the wind who was uncertain if he would let her go or snatch her back.

"Come on."

"Right here."

"Sit this way."

"No, don't lean—like this. Watch me."

"Is this right?"

"That's better."

"Ugh. I feel all scrambled up."

"You'll get used to it."

"Now this is the way you hold your marble."

"How, Bristol?"

"Like this."

"See mine, Becky?" Griffith held up his hand.

"Yes."

"That's right."

"Now, squeeze," Bristol told her.

"How?"

"Like this."

Rebecca squeezed and thumped but the marble only dropped heavily to the ground. The boys exploded into laughter.

"It's not funny," Becky said. "I can't make it come."

"Haha."

"Girl."

"Oh, come on. Help me."

"All right. I'll do it." Bristol cupped his hand over his sister's, took his aim, forced her fingers, and shot. A marble rolled out.

"Good."

"That right?"

"That's fine," Griffith said admiringly.

"OK, I'll do my own."

"Here's your Blue," Bristol said. He handed Rebecca the shiny, round glass ball.

She backed away as he was about to drop it into her outstretched palm.

"No."

"What's wrong?"

"No, I don't want to play."

"But why?"

"Come on, Becky," Griffith begged.

"No, I just don't want to."

The boys, used to Ruben's sudden strangenesses, thought little of their sister's pouting. So they shrugged and gathered up their marbles, stuffing them down deep into their pockets.

They walked on, sometimes playing tag, sometimes follow-the-leader, sometimes close together, sometimes spread apart. They walked across the meadow until they could see the concave flexibility of Passerman's Hollow down beneath them.

"Let's go down," Griffith said.

"There's good grapevines there." Bristol was excited. "This tall." He held his hand as far as it would reach above his head. "You can really swing on 'em." Like a great golden bird on a silver day, like a dream that was born and died in play.

"Let's go," Griffith repeated.

"I don't want to," Rebecca said.

"Why?"

"I just don't!"

"Aw, for pete's sake, Becky."

"I want to go," Griffith said.

"Me, too."

Both boys looked at the girl who as about to spoil their fun.

Rebecca hung her head and said nothing.

"Come on," Bristol tugged at his brother's sleeve.

"Yeah."

"You stay here, then," Griffith told her. "We'll not go far."

Rebecca looked up at him, with tears in her eyes. "All right," she said hoarsely. "I'll go."

Shrugging uncertainly, disappointed because they could not understand her or what had spoiled her fun, Bristol and Griffith started down the steep slope. Rebecca followed, trembling, her ankles turning, her feet slipping. She groped for twigs, branches, rocks to catch herself on. Often she bent double and plodded both hands flat on the ground. She had never been so clumsy.

"Gee, Becky," Griffith complained.

"I'm sorry."

"It's OK, I guess. You're a girl."

Then from somewhere in the densely packed trees in the hollow down there, she heard laughter. She heard it before the boys, and stopped in her tracks, frightened.

The mad, mocking laughter stopped, then started again. This time, both Bristol and Griffith cocked their heads to one side and turned their listening ears windward.

"Woooo," came the sound, like the call of a black night bird from its perch on a high naked bough. "Woooo." And then, shrill, high-pitched laughter, squeaking as it rippled through the leaves and screeched through steel wheeled sunbeams.

"Who's there?" Bristol called, his boyish voice a tremulous whine. "Who's there?"

Griffith, clinging to his brother's arm, echoed "Who's there?" But the echo of his voice came back in ear-splitting laughter. Rebecca covered her face with her hands and pulled her sweater closer to her. "Who's there?" she whispered, but her heart answered, "You know."

Hunky Miller, perched on the low-slung branch of a pawpaw tree, let his arms dangle down in the wind. His face was turned up to the sun, and he was busy counting the colors in the sky: blue, white, yellow. When he squinted his eyes, he made more colors: melon, coral, lemon, raspberry. When he closed them and squeezed them tight, he got shades of black and midnight blue, polka-dotted purple.

Hunky's round legs doubled under him supported his muscular weight. The balls of his feet curved to the branch he was squatting on; his toes turned in like claws. He heard the cries of the children and the mad, nagging laughter of Ruben, but only distantly. He was busy counting the colors of the sky.

On the ground beneath him, Ruben lay writhing in a patch of slick green grass. His jeans had rubbed against the grass until the rough friction had broken down the blades and his bare feet had dug little holes in the soft moldy-smelling ground. Ruben was pounding away on the tiny wilted violets he had torn out with his fingers.

His face was streaked with tears and sweat, his mouth was twisted with the hideous, frightened frothing motions of his tongue against his cheeks and teeth. He rolled his eyes, then shut them, then opened and rolled them.

Hunky, aware that Ruben was in pain, clawed down at the wind with his dangling arms. But Ruben paid him no mind.

Then Hunky said, "They're up there. Can you hear them? They're calling you."

"Wooooo," Ruben moaned, flopping over on his back. "Woooo." And he raked at the air with his arms. "Wooo."

Hunky put one finger in his mouth and chewed on it anxiously. He knew that he was not to leave Ruben. But what was he to do for him? In all the days and nights they had run together like wild animals in these woods, Ruben had never had a spell like this. Sometimes his moodiness had disturbed Hunky, whose quietness was interspersed with hours of teasing and mimicking. But he was sensitive to sadness, and Ruben's depression bothered him.

"Run away, Hunky," he thought. "Run away and look for sunbeams. Look for bright yellow sunbeams."

But his sister Hilda had said, "Watch out for him." And Hunky could not watch out for Ruben unless he were with him.

He brought his eyes down to focus on the wild, obsessed movements of the boy. There was blood mixed with saliva on his chin now. He had gnashed himself when he was crying out. Hunky recoiled at the sight of the young boy's blood. It sickened him. It reminded him of the sun going down, the sun that never promised him it would rise again.

"Ruben," he cried softly. "Ruben?"

But the boy only turned and cried out and moaned.

Hunky shook his head. He would have to get help.

Skinnying up the narrow trunk of the pawpaw tree and peering through its thick clusters of leaves, he saw the three children standing on the bank of the steep hill. "The girl's with them," Hunky saw. "The girl."

He remembered the nights he had spent keeping watch at the foot of the white plank house, stroking the heads and long ears of the hounds so they would not bark, while Ruben sat talking with his sister. He thought of how sad Ruben had been since the girl had lain in her bed sick with fever. If anyone could help with Ruben, it would be Rebecca.

Holding to a high bough with both hands, and pulling up his body into the form of a horseshoe, Hunky swung himself out into the open and hallooed to the three small figures on the hill.

Griffith and Bristol stood frozen, seeing this strange creature appear from the depths of the woods. But Rebecca recognized the husky, hairy, doubled-over figure of Hunky Miller and went running down the hillside to see what it was he wanted.

IX

Rebecca knelt down on the plot of freshly turned ground and put her hands on Ruben's head. The boy opened his eyes and looked up into that glowing oval of calmness, then turned his head to one side and, resting his cheek upon Rebecca's wrist, began to weep.

Hunky waited restlessly, rocking from foot to foot, for Rebecca's commands.

Bristol and Griffith hung back, crouching self-consciously on the heavy gnarled roots of an oak tree, squinting up through the green leafy umbrellas of touching treetops for leaks of sunlight that came drizzling down on their brown arms, splattering them with shadow freckles.

"Ruben," Rebecca whispered. "Ruben, don't cry."

But the boy sobbed harder, curling himself up into a sinewy lump of misery, clutching out at Rebecca with hands that were scratched and torn, bloody from tearing at their own roughness, with half moons of fresh damp earth packed tightly beneath their stubby nails, half moons that flashed and then hid themselves as Ruben clenched and opened his balled-up fists.

Hunky said to Rebecca, "He's been like that all day. Ran off this morning, well before sunup. Could hear him slippin' down the side of the house. Slip-slip-slip. Followed him. Didn't even have my clothes on yet. Grabbed them and carried them over one arm." Hunky's words were short, close clipped, rattled together in his nervous excitement. He waved his arms uncertainly, showing Rebecca how he had glided down the house after Ruben, his shirt and pants wrapped over an arm. Then Hunky looked at himself carefully, making sure he had really taken time to dress.

"Followed him through the meadow," he went on. "He was running like sixty, with that mean look in his eye. Down the hill he came, his arms out in the wind—" and

Hunky dipped his arms up and down like the huge, spread wings of a hawk, to show the children how Ruben had run. "Then I lost him."

Hunky closed both eyes and stretched himself up on his toes, tapping his fingers nervously against the tree. "Lost him, lost him. He ran fast, like a streak of hot sun, flashing across the ground, searing it orange. Orange." And Hunky rolled his tongue against the roof of his dry mouth, tasting the color of the sun burning earth this flashy, fleshy color.

"What did you do?" Rebecca asked.

Hunky bent down and tapped Rebecca lightly on the arm. Then he put his finger over his mouth to show quiet. "I stayed," he said. "I stayed and looked for him for a long time. Because your mother says to watch him."

Hunky's eyes darted quickly, meaningfully between Rebecca and her brother. "Watch him," he repeated. "So I looked for him. I hid in the flowers and waited for him to come and squeeze them open with his little fingers. He didn't come. I got in a rock and waited for him to come and lie down on it. Then I did this," and Hunky whirled himself around and around, his arms clamped down close to his sides. "I turned myself into a tree. A beautiful green tree with lots of low branches. Branches all hooked over so he could climb up them real easy. I waited and waited. I put notches on my trunk so he could go up the hard way. But he didn't come."

Bristol and Griffith, listening to Hunky Miller, kept their faces turned away so he could not see them laughing. Only Rebecca watched her uncle with understanding, tears of pity in her eyes. Ruben, lying still, watched the tears welling up at the edges of her black eyelash frames, like creeks ready to overrun their banks when the next rain fell. Ruben held his breath and forced his body to stop its twitching, he willed himself to be quiet, absolutely still, lest his slightest movement fan the air and bring down a shower of Becky-tears upon him.

"I was a snake," Hunky went on. "A little green snake,

squirmy-squirmy in the grass, slithering along, ready to snare him by the ankles. But no Ruben feet in the grass.

"I talked to the birds. I said 'cheep cheep.' But they were busy, pecking the ground for food." Hunky shook his head sadly, jerking his short stubby neck from side to side in a searching motion. "I couldn't find the little boy, Hilda's little boy."

"Where was he?" Rebecca asked.

Hunky shrugged. "Don't know. Found him following me! Must have been going in circles, because I was. When I turned and saw him—" and here Hunky leaped and stretched out his arms as if he were turning and seeing Ruben crouching low behind him, "he stretched out on the ground and started that moaning. Right here." Hunky stamped his foot on the ground. "Been that way ever since."

Rebecca lifted up Ruben's scratched, tear-swollen face and let his head lie lightly in her lap. "Don't cry," she told him. "Don't cry anymore."

Then she bent down and whispered something to him, whispered too quietly, so softly that not even Hunky's bent ears could catch her words.

Listening, Ruben's forced quiet grew peaceful. His breathing no longer came in short coarse gasps, as if he were rattling for forbidden air, and the splitting agony inside his head grew dimmer and then vanished, leaving him with a deep, sad melancholy instead of the violence that had possessed him only minutes ago.

The violet eyes, brimming with sunny tears, that had awakened him in the night and sucked him into their clear, swirling pools of light, closed gently. Long, brown lashes swept down and sealed the tomb, covering a few cheekbone freckles as they slid into place.

As though he had seen the sun, then shut his eyes and seen a thousand tiny suns dancing before him on the dark earth rotations of his mind, so the round glowing circles of violet reflections danced, then died. Ruben, weak, but no longer frightened, pulled himself up and sat trembling on the grass, trying to bring into focus the blurred image of his sister, Hunky Miller, and the two boys beneath the oak tree.

"We'll take you home now," Rebecca said, when they had waited for the dazed mustard look on Ruben's face to fade and the old sadness-slyness-mockery grin to return to his curled lips.

He clutched at her sweater sleeve, as if to remind her that he could not go home.

"We'll take you to Colby," Hunky signaled with jerks of his head towards Moonridge.

Nodding, Ruben slid off the grass and linked one arm through Rebecca's, one through Hunky's. Bristol and Griffith trailed along behind, stepping lightly through the soft mushy earth.

They walked quietly, not hurrying, not dallying, half pulling, half pushing Ruben up the steep bank of Passerman's Hollow. Once they halted, when Ruben bent down and plucked a violet he had glimpsed beneath a wild strawberry leaf. With a smile, he handed the flower to Rebecca, who tucked it in her jeans' pocket.

On the flat meadow they broke their chain, and Ruben went dashing off through the high grass, his feet charged with speed, flecking up acorns, twigs, torn leaves, whatever lay beneath them in their way. On he galloped, on, on, through brittle bratched wind that struck at him with its claws through islands of sun splashing here and there, bright enough to blind him; on through spider webs permeated with dew, blackberry dew that squashed up between his toes and crept into his blood stream, chilling his poorly tempered body that melted away without so much as a sizzle of protest.

As he ran, the world beneath him spun, stopped, spun backwards, stopped, spun upside down in dizzy whirling, twirling, curling motions. He felt daisy light, scrambling through the air, wafting along with no weightiness to remind him of the true monochrome earth he was bound to, the violet trees and flowers and faces that stared at him so unforgivingly.

Hunky galloped behind, his weight set low against the ground, stampeding the grass with what seemed to him a tortoise pace. His breathing was labored, his eyes were sun glued to the frail dancing shadow of the running Ruben boy.

Rebecca, Bristol, and Griffith stood alone, watching them run toward Moonridge, run their gauntlet of incoherence, striking out with their fleeing feet at all they did not understand, at all they did not want to know.

On their way back, they played leapfrog. Rebecca was best, because she was lightest and her body toughest. The long skinny girlish arms clamped down on her brothers' broad backs and her willowy body sailed over them smoothly. The cotton-dress skirt she had stuffed into her jeans tops flew out and waved beneath her with each leap. The boys laughed to watch their sister go like a kite through the spring-fresh sunlight.

"Leap," Bristol would call.

"Frog!" Griffith screamed.

"Leapfrog!" they would chorus together, and Rebecca would sail, fairy light, through the wind, springing over their crouched-down bodies.

"Leap!"

"Frog!"

"Leapfrog!"

Again, long skinny jumps as she caught her breath sharply and rode the wind.

"Leap!"

"Frog!"

"Leapfrog!"

Tired, giggling, she slipped and went sliding to the grass-textured web of green herb salve that soothed her tired strained muscles and pulled back.

When Bristol took out his marbles and nodded to Griffith that he was ready to play again, Rebecca grabbed playfully for the big Blue he held tightly in his wadded-up fist.

"Here," Bristol gave to her, surprised, and watched her shoot clumsily at Griffith's glass kaleidoscope, laughing when she missed and rolled outside the imaginary circle.

Missed me, missed me, now you have to kiss me. They all laughed.

"I'll show you," Bristol offered, getting ready to take her hand again and show her how to shoot properly.

Rebecca shook her head and motioned to him to leave her alone. She rolled up on the ground, rocking back on her heels, dipping her head down low enough to smudge her chin with fresh dirt. Squinting one eye practicedly, she aimed, rolled the Blue fretfully for a moment, then released it. Griffith's haughty, red-eyed marble sounded a sharp zing! then splintered a blade of grass in its hurry to fly out of range of the big Blue.

"Ha," Rebecca said, satisfied. She handed Bristol back his marble. Tiring of the boys' game, she stretched out in the grass and rolled down the slope. Her body gathered momentum as she glided over bumps and rocks; it flinched when the sharp edges of stones dug into her flesh, and Rebecca smiled, thinking of the small wound she had inflicted upon herself.

Down she went, her blue-jeaned legs thumping against the ground, her yellow hair catching in the high sticky grasses, pulling as it tangled in dewy blobs of wind. Down the hill, turning, turning, turning. Her head grew giddy from the rotations and her thoughts swam into a sea of violet and orange, and bright, busy red, then exploded into streaks of navy, pea green, and russet brown. Her arms stretched out at each side, her legs clamped together, her head thrown back, she lay on her back and glared up at the bright blue windy world that had awakened her from her dizzy dream by stopping her at the bottom of the slope.

On the hill opposite, Crystal Gilbert stood with Phace Adkins beside his parked blue pickup, watching the children running and dancing and kicking up their heels on the north meadow.

"Like wild animals!" Phace roared, spitting his tobacco out into a spittoon of green grass.

"Like calves," Crystal said gently, "like young calves that frisk about on a fine warm day. Let them run, Phace. What difference does it make to you?"

Phace Adkins regarded Crystal Gilbert coldly with his hard, flinty little eyes. "It makes a lot of difference," he said. "My girl Carla's not out there with them."

"Plenty of days your girl Carla ran with them."

"More than she should have," Phace muttered.

"Now, look—" Crystal leaned back, propping his huge bulk on the hood of the truck. "I know how you feel, Phace. I've got a daughter, too. You know Rosie."

Phace nodded.

"How'd you think I'd feel if little Rosie were . . ."

"Murdered," Phace said flatly. "Murdered."

"Not able to be one of them," Crystal went on, watching the children at play on the north meadow. "Well, I'd be wretched. I'd be sick inside. I'd want to pick something up and squeeze it as hard as I could, squeeze the life out of it and then throw it away and watch it bash itself to smithereens against a thick butt of a mute old tree. And maybe I'd pick up whatever was handy—a ball, or an old bone or something like that—and throw it. But I'd not take it out on little kids, Phace. I'd not be bitter because there were other kids left in the world to run and laugh and enjoy the lightness of a spring day."

"I know how you'd feel, Sheriff," Phace said, his voice held down with difficulty. "I tell you exactly how you'd feel. You'd feel walled up with hate and bitterness and anger, not only because of what had happened to your girl, though God knows that's bad enough, but on account of you've got another dead woman on your hands, a wife who just sits in her chair and rocks all day, and won't do nothing but stare at the wall. And on account of you're dead inside, too, dead and mildewy and old before your time, with no hopes for another child or a happy evening around the fire with your family or a warm night in bed with your wife."

Phace stopped and worked his jaw. "And then, when you looked out, and saw them little imps, free as a bird, with their hair a-flyin' in the wind and their chilly little eyes not caring about your suffering, you'd hate the way I do."

"You thinking of doing something, Phace?"

Phace stared hard at the sheriff, and no answer came from his lips or his eyes.

Then the back screen door slammed to. The two men jumped and turned their heads towards the kitchen. There stood Myra Adkins, leaning against a porch post, her hair loose and wild, gleaming in the sunlight. Her arms were clutched up around a bushel basket she was holding.

"What is it, Myra?" Phace cried, sprinting off towards the trembling swaying shadow of the woman who had been his wife for almost twenty years.

"What is it?"

Crystal Gilbert followed close at Phace's heels.

As though she did not see them, Myra answered to the airy patches of bright and darkness that glided before her eyes. "I'm hanging up the wash."

Phace reached for the basket, but Myra's grip could not be pried loose.

"No," she said. "I've done the wash, Phace, and I must hang it up."

The man looked into his wife's face, then peered into the basket.

"But these are Carla's clothes," he cried hoarsely.

"Yes," she said. "I did them in the kitchen sink. Their colors might fade if I put them in the washer. I don't like the way it beats and swishes the life out of things anyway."

Phace reached in the basket and pulled out a soft pink

blouse. He held it up and rolled out the wrinkles Myra's wringing had put into it.

"Isn't it pretty, Sheriff?" he asked meaningfully.

"It's a right pretty blouse," Crystal said.

"I made it for Carla," Myra told whoever was listening, and stepped down off the porch. Phace tried again to take the basket from her, but Myra clung to it with all her strength.

"Can I help you?" Phace asked.

"You can get me the clothespins."

Phace stood beside his wife at the clothesline, bending down into the tomato basket for clothespins whenever Myra held out her hand. But he did not touch the clothes in the basket again. Myra herself pulled them out, shook them, patted them and hung them carefully on the line. If she was not pleased with the way the dresses hung, she took them down, shook them again, and pinned them back, smoothing out sleeves, pulling down skirts, touching each piece of wet, damp cloth with all the love and gentleness that she had once given Carla.

Sitting at the bottom of the hill, Rebecca saw the clothes going up on the line. Shuddering, wrapping her sweater about her, she crept upon a rock and watched the wooden movements of Myra and Phace Adkins as they hung out their washing.

Then she saw Crystal Gilbert standing by his truck. He waved and she waved back, frozenly.

"Who's that?" Bristol asked, running up beside her.

"The sheriff," Griffith answered him, panting hard.

"What's he doing there?"

"Who knows?"

"What's he want?"

"No idea."

"Who's he with?"

"Mr. and Mrs. Adkins."

A pause, then, "What's she doing?"

"Hanging out a wash."

"Whose clothes are those?"

The boys looked at each other, then at Rebecca, and said no more.

The sheriff seemed to be calling to them.

He cupped both hands at his mouth and a gusty hallo rattled in their ears.

"What's he want?" Griffith whispered up to Rebecca.

The girl shook her head.

"Hallooooo."

Rebecca waved back.

Then she saw the sheriff raise one long, bulky arm and motion for them to come on down.

She, Griffith and Bristol went slowly down the hill and climbed up the other side to Phace Adkins' house.

"What'd you call them over here for?" Phace snapped. "I don't want them hanging around."

"They won't be hanging around," Crystal said evenly. "But I want to talk to them. The girl's been sick. I'm glad to see her out again."

"Humph."

"Be civil, Phace," the sheriff told the angry-looking man. "After all, isn't this what you wanted?"

Phace said nothing, but turned on his heel and walked away. Myra stood woodenly, waiting for a clothespin.

Then Rebecca was there to stoop to the tomato basket and hand her one.

"That was Carla's job," Myra Adkins said, by way of greeting.

"It's mine, too," Rebecca said.

"Be glad," Myra told her from between clenched teeth. She was holding a blue dress by the collar while she separated the skirt from its sewn-in petticoat. Straight pins were still stuck in the hem, and a loose thread was raveling from the sleeve.

Rebecca began to pick out the pins.

"I didn't get it quite finished," Myra Adkins said, as she yanked off the thread. "Did I?"

"Is this new?" Rebecca asked.

"Yes. I made a dress for Carla. Just like the one her daddy got her. The blue one she wore to her birthday party."

"How've you been?" Crystal asked when the children had been taken inside and set down around the kitchen table with a glass of milk each and a plate of sugar cookies.

"OK," Bristol said, licking off the moustache of sweet milk from his upper lip.

"Fine," Griffith grunted, reaching for another cookie.

"And you, Rebecca?"

"All right," Rebecca said, staring at her hands.

"The fever's gone?"

"I guess so."

"You'll be back in school Monday?"

"If Mom says I can go."

"Don't walk to the bus alone," Myra said.

"We go together, Mrs. Adkins," Rebecca reached up shyly and touched the woman's still limp hand, a hand that was red and chapped from working with wet clothes in the wind.

"How's your mom and pa?" Phace said studiedly. "I've not seen them much lately."

"Dad's fine," Rebecca rushed out the words. "He's been busy this week. He'll stop by soon. Mom's not feeling too well—and she's been staying in close with me. I expect she'll be over now, too."

"Must be the fever," Crystal commented.

"Uh-huh."

"I'm glad she stays in with you," Myra said. "I don't like the thoughts of you alone in that big house."

Rebecca smiled but said nothing.

"How's Ruben?" Crystal asked.

"He's all right," Bristol said, eyeing the plate of cookies.

"He's gone over to stay with Colby Chaser for a while," Rebecca told them as she picked up her milk and took a big gulp.

"Your grandpa not well?"

"No, I think he's all right. He just likes Ruben. Says he's good company."

"How long will the boy stay there?"

"I don't know," Rebecca said. "As long as he wants to stay, I guess. Or as long as Colby wants him there."

"Doesn't he get homesick?"

Rebecca shook her head and pushed back a wisp of yellow hair. "It's not far from home."

"It sure isn't," Phace Adkins said. "Do you visit often?"

"Not much. I've been sick. And there's school."

"How about Ruben?" Phace asked.

The children said nothing.

"I saw you all on the meadow this morning," Phace said challengingly. "There were five of you. I'll bet that Hunky Miller was along."

"Yes, he was," Rebecca said. "Well, we've got to go. Thanks for the milk and cookies." She slid from her chair and dashed through the screen, Bristol and Griffith close behind her. The door slammed to with a bang that echoed the glare Crystal Gilbert gave Phace Adkins.

"You scared them," the sheriff said. "You scared them. You fool."

X

Sheriff Gilbert's little blue pickup in the driveway sent Hunky Miller scooting to his room, motioning frantically to Ruben to look out the window. But the boy was already there, flattening his face against the pane, his ears perked up to catch the wind as it sifted through the glass. Ripples of sunlight bounced from the brown shingled roof to his taut, drawn-in cheeks, playing a momentary game of hide-and-seek, crossing his eyes, nose, mouth and the light hairs of the moustache now thick above his lips. He dazzled, he was a prism of colors sifting through the windowpane and Hunky Miller thought, for just a moment, that he had found the rainbow.

There was a heavy knock on the door. Colby Chaser put up the rifle he was cleaning and reached for his cane. "Who's there?" he called out.

"Crystal Gilbert." The sheriff's voice was steady and loud.

"Come on in, Crys. You don't have to knock." The old man settled down in his chair again.

"Much obliged." Crystal pushed open the door and blinked at the dimness of the kitchen-sitting room where Colby made himself at home.

"How've you been?" the sheriff asked.

"Good enough. Can't complain with a leg like this." And Colby patted his bent right leg. "It knows everything, good weather, bad, hunting days, walking days—even tells me when I'm having company—by the vibrations from the road. They come up my toes." And Colby grinned foxily at Crystal.

"So you knew I was coming?" the big man asked, settling himself into a hard-bottomed, straight-back chair.

"Sure. I knew you'd come. Like I said, I felt the vibrations."

"Uh-huh. When'd they start, Colby?"

"That's hard to say," the old man chortled. "I can't pick up vibrations on a day like this until I hear you coming up the hill. Especially if you haven't telephoned first."

"Oh."

"Not much magic, huh?"

"I wouldn't say that."

Crystal began to focus on the cluttered-up, unswept room. He saw stacks of Colby's hunting magazines under the windows, boxes of bullets, old gun parts thrown around, piles of dirty rags, spread-out newspapers yellowed from age, shoe-shining polish, a clock that was half put back together, a dirty bowl with cat's milk sloshed out on the linoleum-covered floor.

"Who's doing your housekeeping?" Crystal asked.

Colby smiled and fiddled with the buttons on his plaid shirt. "Hilda usually does for me," he said. "But she's not been over this week."

"Oh."

"Her girl's had the fever. So I had to reconcile myself to settle back and enjoy the mess while it lasted. And not have company."

Crystal acknowledged by a smile that he had been put in his place. "Well, this is not a social call, Colby," he said.

"Business, then?"

"More or less. Not official, though."

"Oh? How's that?"

"I've come to see Ruben Lawson."

There was a pause and then the slick, spitty sound of Colby's tongue gliding across his yellow teeth. "Oh?" he said at last.

"Yes."

"What about?"

Crystal said nothing.

"I'm the boy's grandpa," Colby barked. "You may as well say to me."

"Sure. But I'd just as soon see Ruben and tell you both at once."

Hunky was gesturing towards the window, grunting heavily in wordless agitation to indicate that Ruben should pull loose the panes of glass and slip away. But the boy, his eyes burning with excitement and curiosity, shut Hunky out of his thoughts; he leaned over the stair railings and hung on to each word exchanged in the room below.

There was fear in Hunky's eyes as he watched Ruben, fear of something he did not grasp. The animal fright was instinctive, and his urge was to protect: himself, his house, his stepfather, the boy his sister had handed over to him. They must be protected from the strange new power permeating the house in the strange new smell of Crystal Gilbert. Hunky stretched out one arm and let his granite grasp come to rest on Ruben's wrist.

Ruben stared angrily at Hunky, raising his free hand to strike. His face was a scar of mixed feelings. He understood Hunky's reactions; he too felt the new power, smelled the new smell of something akin to forcefulness; he felt danger, he felt Hunky's fear and instinctive need to protect. For a moment he hesitated, then curiosity overcame him. He tensed his wrist muscles, then relaxed them, contracting his arm until he could jerk it loose from Hunky's grip. Then he scooted down the banister, leaving Hunky stuttering inarticulately, and stood at the landing, face to face with Crystal Gilbert.

"I was just coming to call you," Crystal said.

"I heard."

"You're a prompt boy."

"I try to be."

"You're fast, too."

Ruben looked directly at the sheriff. He felt Hunky's shadow above him, stretching out over his head. Hunky was listening and watching. "What'd you want?" he said.

The sheriff smiled. "You remember the day I came to see your family?" he asked. "You and your brothers were at work on the barn. Cleaning it."

Ruben nodded.

"I told you that day I might need a deputy. You said you'd be interested. Remember that?"

"Oh, yes."

"Well," Crystal smiled, "I need one now. See, nobody's with me." He jerked his head in the direction of the empty pickup. "I've got nobody to scrape the mud off my truck and drive me back and forth when I need to be taken."

"Uh-huh." Ruben's eyes shone.

"Can you drive?"

"Oh, yes."

"Your daddy teach you?"

"Yes."

"Got your license?"

The boy's face fell.

"No mind. We can fix that up. Where'd you learn to drive?"

"At home."

"On your pa's truck?"

"Uh-huh."

"Swell. Know anything about cars?"

"A little."

"Know where everything is—engine, tires, brakes? Know the gearshift? Can you change a tire?"

"Uh-huh."

"You got to keep my truck clean."

"All right."

"Good. You're hired."

"I'm a deputy?"

"Let's say you're assistant deputy. Until my regular men get back. One's got the flu, the other went to visit his sister in Chardon. She'd been having a little marriage trouble and asked him to come over and help her out. So he asked off a week or so. I need a good man for at least six or seven days."

"That's fine," Ruben grinned.

"What about pay?" Colby asked, his beady blue eyes flashing.

"What about it, Ruben?"

Ruben waved his hand to say that it did not matter.

"No, no, that's not the right attitude, boy," Colby Chaser said. "If you're going to work for the sheriff, if you're going to put your hours in, you might as well draw your pay same as anybody else."

"That's right, Colby," Crystal agreed.

"Just good business," Colby said.

Ruben licked his lips eagerly.

"How about fifty dollars for the week?"

Hunky, watching from his perch on the banister, signaled Ruben that he should ask for more. But the boy shook his head and said, "Fifty's fine." Fine, he thought. What did money matter to him? All he wanted was the star, he told Crystal Gilbert pleadingly.

"Star?" Crystal was puzzled.

"Uh-huh."

"Well, I'll see what I can do. You want a star, you say?"

Ruben nodded.

"How about a badge?"

Ruben hung his head and his lower lip quivered.

"No badge, huh? It has to be a star."

Ruben darted a quick look at the sheriff.

"All right," Crystal said. "All right, I'll get you a star."

❊   ❊   ❊

"Ruben," he heard the voice calling. "Ruben, Ruben."

Buried beneath his pillow and clenched hands, he pressed his head down into the deep feather bed he shared with Hunky and cocked his ears into the pitch-black fluffiness of the mattress.

"Ruben, Ruben."

"Oh," he mumbled.

"Ruben."

The call was clear and struck terror into his boiling body. But the voice was confused, it was a mingling of childishness and maturity, of highballed laughter and dejection, of pity and of passion.

Then came the eyes, quivering, pulsating, flashing this way and that, beneath the sheets, beneath the pillow, on the ceiling, on the floor, up and down the walls like frenzied knocking spirits.

"Uh," Ruben groaned, and pushed himself deeper and deeper into the warm, sweaty thickness of the bed, pushed himself farther away from the heat of Hunky's bulky body, closer to the coolness of the air-washed edge of the bed.

The eyes followed him here, and the voice came closer on the air he stirred by his frantic motions. The eyes hovered above him, calling, staring, parching him of the water content of his body by their strange siphoning suction.

Likewise also these filthy dreamers defile the flesh.

He could not cry out, because he was breathless, intoxicated by the lightness of his body, his mind, his being. He was stunned, he was suffocating, he staggered beneath the weightiness of the vamping spirit. It robbed him of his voice, his sight—and he could not tell who it was, there in the darkness, staring at him out of those colorless eyes, calling to him from the lipless mouth. He lay in terror, in fear, until, encircling him, gripping him, squeezing him, those eyes forced him to eject even these emotions and then went away, exuding the sweat and sticky awe they had drained him of.

He rested for a while, his head on his folded arms, sobbing quietly into his cupped hands. Then he roused himself to the side of his bed and sat, static, reviving in the cool air.

"Uh," he sighed, and slipped up, his light feet barely skimming the floor as he dashed to the window.

"Who's there?"

Hunky Miller stuttered, drawing up his muscular body in time to see Ruben pulling on his jeans in a quick hurried movement, stretching his right leg out the window as he pulled on the zipper, jerking his left leg through behind, skinnying down the boards and rainpipe in one swift, supple, elastic stretch.

"Gone!" Hunky, no longer grinning to himself, heard only his own catch-as-catch-can intake of breath, his plummeting heart in his rib-notched chest. He leaped from the mattress, grabbed for his clothes, and followed Ruben through the window, scrambling down the side of the house and taking off in a bulldog run at the heels of the dervish Ruben.

They ran with great beauty, their heads thrown back into the clear spring night air, their eyes on a thick, yellow curdled moon that watched them relentlessly from her perch on a china-thin cloud. Their arms were lifted up and out at their sides as if to propel them, like the great spread wings of invisible night birds flapping, flapping, flapping in their hush-hush hegira into the unknown.

Flowers beneath their feet ebbed courteously, then sprang back in ecstatic ripples. Foaming grasses, pressed down, rose steadily in right-to-left evolutions of revival. The wind, cut through by their swiftness as a slab of freshly molded butter by a sharp knife, cringed, wrinkled, then snapped back from spliced fragments into a trembling whole that swept the fields of Moonridge with iridescent waves of golden glory.

They ran, as two wild young things run when they pursue and are pursued, when they retreat and are retreated from. From Moonridge, and its fastidious collection of trees, flowers, grasses, knolls, fences, and moonlit master fields, to the white plank house where all the lights were snuffed but the one in Rebecca's room.

Hunky's whistle alerted the girl. She threw on her pink cotton robe and cracked the door so Ruben could slip in.

He came, panting hard, his hair slick and sticking to his head, his eyes round and wild with some new glow that, for the first time, frightened Rebecca. His hands were trembling, and the skin torn from them in his hurried climb up the side of the house either gapped loose or was missing. The window of his room had been boarded up again, and he had had to tear off the planks and pull out the nails, one by one, sticking them between his teeth so they would not fall and clink against the roof. This time his pa had hammered their steely little heads deep, and Ruben had torn loose a fingernail as he grubbed away with his bare hands.

Rebecca let out a little whimpering cry when she saw his hands. Ruben tucked them behind his back, ashamed of having frightened her, and smiled in the old friendly way. He stood waiting for little Becky to bring out the jar of vaseline salve she now kept in her own dresser drawer.

"I come to tell you," he whispered, as she dressed his hands.

"What?"

"I had company today."

"Who?" Rebecca asked, alarmed.

"Guess!"

Rebecca drew up her legs and shriveled in her shoulders, feeling cold from her brother's damp body. "I don't know."

"Friend of yours."

Still she did not know.

"Rosie's father."

"Crystal Gilbert?"

"The sheriff!"

"What'd he want?" Rebecca wanted to shout, "What'd he want with you, Ruben?" But her heart only beat double time as she stared into her brother's face.

"He came to hire me," Ruben said, quivering with pleasure.

"What?"

"To hire me. As a deputy."

"Oh, Ruben."

"He did. I'm hired. I'm a deputy. I get a star, and fifty dollars a week."

"Oh, Ruben."

"He said he needed men. Somebody to drive his truck.

I got the job. I'm a deputy." Ruben beamed and waited for his sister's praise to be showered down on him.

But "Oh, Ruben," was all she could say.

"Don't you see, little Becky?" he climbed up on her bed, from his squatting position on the floor. He sat cross legged, humped over, quavering with excitement. "Don't you see? A deputy! I'll go to town every day. Maybe live there. I'll see the stores—not just the windows, but the insides. I'll talk to the town people. They'll have plenty to say to me, once they see I'm a man, a deputy. I'll eat at the restaurants all the time. Order from a menu. It's a good thing I can read. I'll bunk at the jail, even . . . woooooo." And he leaned over closer to Rebecca. "I'll even help capture criminals," he said, "and solve cases!"

Rebecca shook her head.

"What's wrong, little Becky?"

"No," she whispered.

"What's wrong? Don't you like it?"

"No," she said. "No, it's not that. I like it, Ruben, I guess. It's just that—it's different. I mean, we're different. We're country people. We don't belong in town. Living in a jail . . . eating in a restaurant."

"What's wrong with that? Restaurant food's good."

"No, it's not."

"How would you know? You've never been in one!"

"Yes, I have."

"When?" Ruben was alert and interested, forgetting his anger at Rebecca.

"Not too long ago," Rebecca's eyes shone with provocation.

"When?"

"In the fall. We slipped off after school, before the bus came, and went in one. We bought a hot dog and french fries."

"You didn't!"

"Yes, I did!"

105

"Where'd you get the money?"

"Saved it."

"How'd you know where to go?"

"*She* told me." Rebecca said. "She found out where other kids went."

"Does Pa know?"

"No!"

"He'd not like it."

"I know."

"He might whip you."

"He might."

And they both giggled. Then Ruben looked at Rebecca seriously. "Why'd you say that, Becky?" he asked. "Why'd you say I'd not like it?"

"Oh, I don't know, Ruben," she said. "But the food's not as good as Mom's. And you have to sit at a counter, I guess, and eat off other people's plates with forks and knives you're not sure as have been washed. And you have to pay for your food as soon as you eat it and get up and go so someone else can have your seat."

"Aw, I don't care," Ruben said after a while. "Besides, there's more to it than that. There's the money. There's fifty dollars, Becky!"

"Do you want the money, Ruben?"

"No." Ruben squeezed his sore hands. "No. But Colby Chaser said I was to take it, he said it was only good business. I don't need the money. It's for you, though. For you. I'll buy you things with the money. Beautiful things. Things you want. Dresses, ribbons, stuff like that."

"No."

"Becky, I'll bring you anything you like. I'll bring you another hot dog!"

"No," she said quickly, and turned her head, hurt.

"Then you can have the money!" Ruben's voice was an angry whisper. "You can have it! I don't want it!"

"No." Rebecca buried her face in her hands.

"What's wrong?" Ruben tapped her shoulder timidly.

"Nothing, brother," she said slowly. "I just don't want you to go."

"Why?" Ruben asked simply.

"I don't know. I guess because I'll miss you."

"No, you won't. I'll wave to you when you go by on the schoolbus. I'll stand outside the sheriff's office and wave. Like this." Ruben pulled himself up straight, stood on the bed and waved grandly. "And I'll sneak back at night. I can bring the truck. Or I'll walk. It's not far. It won't take me long. I'll come, Becky. You know I will."

"But, Ruben," she started to say, "it's not that. I'm afraid!" Instead she only shook her head and said, "It won't be like old times!"

"Bosh!" said Ruben. "It'll be better. I'll be a deputy. I'll have exciting things to tell you. Things about the people and the town and the stores and what I learn. I'll have new things to show you. I'll slip them out to you. When there's real excitement, little Becky, I'll come back for you—take you with me—so you can be in on it, too. Especially if it's at night. Or I'll come in the day, after school. They'll let you go with me!"

"No," Rebecca said slowly, "No, I don't want to."

Angrily, Ruben looked down on the yellow hair and soft blue eyes.

"Why?"

This time she said it. "I'm afraid."

Ruben drew himself up quietly, sprang from the bed to the floor, turned on his heel and sped from the room without uttering another word. He only gave his sister a look of disgust and hurt and disappointment, a look that reproached her for harboring the one emotion he could not tolerate in her.

Yea, what clearing of yourselves, yea, what indignation, yea, what fear, yea, what vehement desire, yea, what zeal, yea, what revenge!

Rebecca followed him, clawing at the wind he kicked up in his mad flight.

"Wait," she whispered. "Wait."

But he was gone, out the window, down the house and running with Hunky Miller towards Moonridge.

"Oh, wait," Rebecca sighed. "I wanted to kiss you good-by."

XI

Rebecca lay in her bed, complaining of a return of the fever. Her face was flushed a brilliant soapy pink, her eyes were bright, burning blue, large and spongy, soaked up with sadness and misery.

Her father brought her a glass of ice water and a cold washrag for her forehead. He took away her schoolbooks and told her to rest.

"Please, Pa," she begged him, "let me have them." Her restless hands were aching for something to occupy them, her mind needed to skip from addition to subtraction, from multiplication to division. She wanted to hold her books and papers and pencils. She wanted to touch the past and know it was still there.

"You need to rest more," Mason Lawson said as he left the room.

Hilda sat at the breakfast table, her eyes focusing on the oilcloth, her head down. She was toying with her breakfast of chopped-up oatmeal, dry toast and black bitter coffee.

"Boys gone?" Mason asked, sitting back down at the table and pouring himself some coffee.

"They were late," Hilda mumbled. "They had to run for the bus."

The sunlight dancing in and out through the window seared Mason's face bright yellow and then went on to play with the wrinkles and redness of Hilda's hands. Hilda looked at the lines on Mason's face and the roughness of her own hands. We're old, she thought. It was only yesterday that we were young, and now we're old. We're too old to sit here doing the same things we did fifteen years ago—and yet here we are, the same as ever. And I've not changed at all inside. I still feel exactly the same towards him and this life as I did when he brought me to this house. Time didn't bring peace, and God didn't do much to help.

"Oh, well," she said aloud, and blinked back tears.

"Try to eat," Mason said, humbly.

Hilda glared at him, then took up a bite of cereal which she held in her mouth a long time before swallowing.

"I won't be gone far today," Mason said, "in case you need me."

And the eye cannot say unto the hand, I have no need of thee: nor again the head to the feet, I have no need of you.

"I won't need you."

"I meant—with Rebecca sick again."

"We won't need you."

"Anyway, I won't be far. I'm going to the back garden to work."

"All right."

"If you feel like it, I wish you'd walk out sometime and see how things are growing. It's so pretty now!"

Yes, Hilda thought. Spring is pretty, spring is life, spring is growing things. Spring is green and yellow, gardens sprouting, grass growing, the sun getting warmer, the wind softer. Spring is children playing. And parents laughing.

But she said nothing.

"Only if you feel like it," Mason repeated.

"I'll see."

I also will laugh at your calamity; I will mock when your fear cometh.

Mason sipped his coffee, Hilda munched on some dry toast. Both tried to think of things to say or not to say to the other.

Then there was the sound of a car in the distance, a car on the dirt road, a car beneath the morning apricot-streaked sky, a car winding between fields and fences. Mason, pre-occupied with his own thoughts, had a fleeting recollection of the schoolbus stopping at the foot of the hill for Bristol and Griffith. Then his mind came back to Hilda, so brooding, so ingrown, so distant to him now. Mona, he remembered, Mona. Was this the way she had gotten? Colby had told them so, but Mason had never believed him. What if it was the truth?

And Cain said unto the Lord, my punishment is greater than I can bear.

The car was nothing to Hilda but the sound of motion on a stagnant day, the sound of other people living, breathing, walking, driving, going places and doing things, mingling in the musty, mountainous preoccupation of doing and being done for. Other men, other creators, other gods—with other women who waited, servile and set upon, to do their pleasure and their bidding at the time they would choose.

She spat out her toast and stared at Mason.

A knock at the door roused them both. Stunned, they looked at each other, then at the door. Hilda was mute. Mason, stirring from his pondering, cried, "Yes?"

Crystal Gilbert asked to be let in.

Scraping his chair legs on the floor, Mason let down his weight and got up to walk slowly to the door. He pulled open the screen with a wooden hand.

"Morning," he said, "come in."

"Thank you, thank you," Crystal answered in a hearty voice.

Hilda rallied to drag herself to the cabinets. She searched for a cup, then poured the sheriff a cup of coffee, then had to pour another because she had not taken out a clean cup.

"That's all right, Cousin Hilda," Crystal said. "That's all right."

Hilda nodded.

"Fine morning," Crystal said. "Going to make a lovely day."

"Yes."

"Fine day for working out."

"Yes."

111

"You going gardening, Mason?"

"That's right."

"Have a good garden this year?"

"A good one. My best, I think."

"Glad to hear it. I like to see green things growing."

"So do I," Mason said, becoming more animated. "I've been telling my wife there, I want her to come out and look it over. She'll be pleased."

"Yes, Mrs. Mason," Crystal said. "How are your flowers?"

"My flowers?"

"Yes—you were working on them the last time I was here."

"Oh, those," Mason cried. "You'll have to look at them, Sheriff. They're beauties."

There was a pause, then Crystal said, "I've got news for you folks. A surprise."

Hilda stared hollowly at the sheriff. She stared at him, through him, through the kitchen wall and out into the green spring world. She looked hard, but she could not see.

Mason finally managed to ask, "What's that?"

"You'll have to see for yourself."

"All right."

Crystal rared back in the seat, letting two legs of the chair fly off the floor. Teetering to and fro, digging hard in the linoleum floor to maintain his balance, Crystal raised his voice and called out, "All right."

The door opened again, slowly, slowly, and this time Ruben Lawson entered the room.

"Ohhh," Hilda cried out, and dropped her coffee spoon. It went clinking to the floor and bounced against Crystal Gilbert's heavy shoe. The sheriff came down with a bang.

Mason's eyes grew large with fright, then quickly contracted when he saw the boy was dressed smartly in a green shirt, green twill pants, dark-brown tie—and a yellow star pinned to the breast pocket of his shirt.

"Well, well," Mason said, standing up and looking the boy over. "Well, well."

Hilda smiled weakly.

"Do you know this young man?" Crystal asked heartily.

"No, no, I don't believe I do," Mason said, carrying the game on. "How about you, honey?"

Startled, cringing as if a blow would follow the "honey," Hilda looked up at her husband, then over at her son. "No?" she said uncertainly.

"No's the right answer," Crystal laughed. "Nobody knows this young man. I brought him by to introduce you to him. This here is Deputy Lawson. Hired for the week to replace two good men who had to be off and just starting work today."

Mason grinned proudly at the boy.

"You look grand, son," he said at last. "You look grand."

"Yes." Hilda seemed to have regained her balance. "You look fine, Ruben."

"I'm proud of you, boy," Mason said.

"So am I," Crystal chimed in. "He looks like he's going to be a fine help. He's a grand driver. Good company. I'm real pleased."

"I'm glad," Mason said. "So glad."

"It was kind of lonely, down there all by myself," Crystal went on. "Yes sir, I just decided to hire me a good man to help out. I think I found one."

Ruben's eyes flashed delightedly and he let the stiffness go from his back for just a moment, long enough for him to bask in the praise he was unused to.

I am beautiful, he thought, yes, I am beautiful. I, too, am a golden-haired boy set free to fly the day on angel's wings. I am beautiful and grand and fine; the world is mine and I am free with a star to protect me.

"Just look at him," Mason said, half aloud, half to himself. "Just look at him, standing there like he was a real deputy, a real law man."

I will heal their backsliding, I will love them freely; for mine anger is turned away from him.

"Yes." Crystal drained the last of his coffee, and refused

the second cup Hilda was ready to pour him. "No, no thanks," he said.

"Well, Sheriff," Mason said. "We can relax here, on East Fork, when we know we have such fine lawmen protecting us."

Crystal Gilbert laughed hard and came down again on the floor from his perch on two legs. "Glad to hear that, Mason," he said, chuckling. "Glad to hear that. Well, we've got to be going. I just dropped by to show you your boy— thought you'd be proud of him."

"We sure are," Hilda said.

"Sure," Mason agreed. "Sure, Crystal. Thanks a lot."

"Just a minute." Hilda got up, seeing the green spring world suddenly inside her kitchen. "Just a minute. Rebecca's home today. She's got the fever again. Let me go see if she doesn't want to come down and look at her brother in his pretty uniform."

"All right," Crystal said. "We can wait."

Hilda climbed the stairs slowly and walked softly down the pine hall. She knocked timidly at Rebecca's door.

"Becky," she called. "Becky, come down and see who's here."

Rebecca said nothing.

"Becky?" Hilda called. "Becky?"

Silence.

Hilda pushed open the door.

Inside, Rebecca was still and quiet in her bed. The cover was stretched over her tightly from head to foot.

"Come see who's downstairs," Hilda repeated softly. "Come on, Becky. It's Ruben."

At the sound of his name, Rebecca threw off the cover and rose up passionately. Her face was flushed, her eyes were burning. "I don't want to," she hissed. "I don't want to see him."

Hilda drew back from the angry sizzling of her daughter's voice, back from her little forked tongue, her flushed pink cheeks, the tears streaming down her face and onto her gown, her bedcovers and the doll she was clutching behind her back.

She closed the door, trembling, and went shakily back to the kitchen. On the way down the stairs, when she stopped once and closed her eyes, she thought she glimpsed roses and violets and white peonies growing on the stairwell.

"Becky isn't feeling up to it," she apologized to Crystal Gilbert. "I shouldn't have gone for her."

And then she noticed that Ruben was gone.

They were quiet, Hilda and Mason, saying little to each other. The shock and fear had subsided, they were relaxed although still on edge and full of guilty suspicions. And now they felt their energy spent. Their arms dangled lifelessly, their legs trembled beneath the table leaves, their minds swirled with new and bewildering thoughts.

Hilda sipped at her cold coffee.

Mason drank more of his, stirring in teaspoonsful of heavy cream.

When he saw that she was about to be sick, Mason helped his wife to the bathroom and stood awkwardly outside the door, waiting for her to come out.

Hilda, thinking of the coffee and the spoon shoveling cream, retched again, choking as she felt the hot nausea boiling up her throat. Then she leaned against the cool windowpane and watched the rain fall, trying not to think of the boy in the green uniform or the girl crying in her bed.

Woe to the crown of pride, she thought suddenly.

Hadn't she known it would rain today?

She heard Mason mumbling, but she shut out the sound of his voice as she leaned against the frosty chill of the window and listened to the plink-plinking of soft rain soaking into velvet grasses. The strawberry sun climbed higher, higher still over silhouettes of plant-leaf trees that promised warmth and richness from the spring-stirred earth. Seeds would ripen, tender shoots would open and something fresh and new would be born, something unspoiled by the ravages of winter and the tears of men's sharp-bladed hoes. Something new and good that she could put her hands on and hold to before any other human touched it and robbed it of its samson-strength.

As newborn babes, desire the sincere milk of the word, that ye may grow thereby: If so be ye have tasted that the Lord is gracious.

She relaxed.

The Lord was gracious, although she didn't always understand Him. The Lord was gracious, although He didn't always help the way she wished He would. But even though she didn't understand Him, He understood her. He had shown her spring, and the freshness of life and given her new growth in a new green world. She would survive, by her own hand and by His.

And then she heard Mason's voice.

"I know it's tough," he was whispering through the closed bathroom door. "I know it is, honey. But we'll manage. God will see us through. I've talked to Him! I've prayed to Him! I've asked Him for help. And don't you worry—He'll see us through!"

She saw the rain had stopped. The ground, saturated, had turned back the last of its tiny drops and they lay, splotchy and muddy, in puddles snaked through the grass. The fragile grasses, the delicate shoots that were raising their sleep-bent heads on tender bodies to awaken to life and the beauty of being, now sagged, washed out, bent over, in a soggy earth that gave way and let their roots slide meaninglessly.

"Don't you worry, honey. God will see us through. Besides, the boy really did look fine. I was proud of him."

Leaning her head back just in time, Hilda was sick again, sick from the words "honey" and "God" and the meek, groveling man who stood whispering them to her through the door he would not open.

XII

"Tell me, boy," Crystal Gilbert said, as Ruben drove the little blue pickup slowly off the rain-slick hill. "Tell me what you think about the law."

Ruben grinned, and tried not to bounce too hard on the deep gash ruts, or drive too fast. He knew Hunky was following through the trees, following until they came to a flat place where he could crawl up in the bed and ride unseen to town.

"The law," Ruben said, rolling the word on his tongue, caressing it, "is a pretty star. A golden star. A yellow star. I've got it, right here." And he patted the tin, pointed star on his shirt.

"It's cold metal that gets hot in the sun, like this truck. It's something you have to keep after—to shine, and polish and rub on, so it won't tarnish. And it has a lot of points to it. A lot of different points. Some of them are pretty sharp."

"Uh-huh," Crystal nodded. "What about my badge, Ruben? Isn't it the law, too?"

Ruben eyed the nondescript shapeless badge the sheriff wore pinned loosely to his jacket.

"I dunno," he said. "I guess so. Maybe it's one of the points." And he smiled happily.

Crystal Gilbert said nothing else. He looked from his right-hand window at East Fork disappearing behind him, its high hills, winding roads, big-bellied creeks flattening into a forgotten perspective as Ruben drove them on towards town. He could still glimpse the outlines of houses, perched tenuously on flanks of mud and rock. Here and there, specks of sunlight made a treetop give out a glowing look of a perfumed cheek flattened against the blue-haired sky.

On the hard road, with Hunky safely flattened out in the

bed behind, Ruben opened up the truck and sped on towards town. On his left and his right, houses gave way to more houses, mailboxes, grocery stores, filling stations, used car dumps, flat, uncleared land, and houses going up with the sound of hammer on nail and plank falling in beside plank.

Crystal took out a little blue notebook from his pocket and pulled a pen from his jacket. He began to scribble.

"Whatcha doing?" Ruben asked.

"Writing."

"Huh. What for?" Ruben's face was friendly, inquisitive.

"I'm making notes to myself."

"Oh."

"I have to do that so I'll remember things. They can slip right by, you know."

"I guess so."

"Would you like to read them? They're official."

"I can't do it," Ruben shook his head. "I'm driving."

"Oh." Crystal fell silent and went back to his scribbling. Ruben's eyes darted from road to notebook, and the boy was a mirror of curiosity.

"Oh, well. I'll tell you what I put down, if you're interested. Seeing how it's official."

"I'm interested," Ruben promised.

"I was adding up figures."

"You don't say!"

"Yes. Reward money."

"Reward?"

"Uh-huh."

"What for?"

"Oh, some of the fellows on East Fork and Fancy Creek and hereabouts—even some of the town folk—put in money to give to a fine, outstanding man."

"Who's that?"

"They don't know."

"Don't know?"

"Huh-uh."

"How come?"

"The money's for the man who can help us."

"Help who?"

"Me, and you, too, now that you're the Law."

"We need help?"

"We sure do!"

"What for?"

"Why, to help us find Carla Adkins."

"Oh, yes."

"Anyway," Crystal Gilbert went on, "this money is reward money for whoever can help us track the girl down."

"I see."

"It isn't much money yet, just $175. But folks around here are farmers. They don't have much to spare."

"No."

"One hundred and seventy-five dollars isn't a bad haul, though."

"No."

"Of course, there's more to it."

"What's that, Sheriff?"

"Oh, a picture in the paper. You know, big write-up. The reporter coming to interview you. Meeting your family, seeing where you live, what you're like, what you do. Folks are going to want to know all these things, folks always want to know all about important people. Free copies of the paper for your friends. Probably a big banquet at the grade school, speeches and the presentation of the reward money. A nice dinner at one of the restaurants in town for the family. All free, of course. Best meal in town on the house! Then a lot of people who couldn't chip in with cash will give presents—"

"You don't say."

"Yes, I've got a promise of a pair of leather boots from McCubbin's store, a smoked ham from the Meek's grocery, a week's free gasoline at Elmer's filling station. Maybe even an honorary badge or star from the state. Since whoever helps us will really be a lawman. What do you think of that, Ruben?"

"Good idea," the boy said, whetting his lips.

"Well, I'm glad you think so. I'll add the honorary star to the list of prizes. You really think it's a good idea?"

"Yes."

"Well, good."

There was silence for the next five miles. Then Crystal Gilbert asked, "By the way, Ruben, I don't think I ever told you my arrangements."

"How's that?"

"My arrangements. How I live."

"Oh. No, you haven't, Sheriff."

"Well, I sleep at the jail when I'm busy and can't get home at nights. I have a nice little cot all fixed up there. One of my deputies does, too. You can have his. The wife takes care of them for us. Clean sheets and all that. Then, I eat at the diner. Lunch and supper. Can't really barge in on the wife when I'm busy and she wouldn't know when to expect me. Breakfast I do myself—coffee, toast, an egg. Sound all right to you?"

"Sounds fine," Ruben said.

"Something else I need to ask you," Crystal said suddenly.

"What's that?"

"How're you fixed for cash?"

"Hum?"

"Don't you need some money? In advance, that is? You have to pay for your meals, you know—oh, we get special lunch prices, but dinner's on your own."

"I guess I've got enough."

"How much?"

"Two dollars."

"Maybe I'd better advance you a little."

"I don't really want—"

"Oh, come on, boy. Every young man wants him some pocket money. It makes him feel good to have a little loose to spend—get himself a haircut, a soda, things like that."

"I guess so."

"You might even want to pick up a little something for your girl."

"No. I don't have one."

"Well, for your mom, then."

"Yeah, maybe."

"I'll advance you five dollars."

"All right, Sheriff."

"I'll bet it won't be any time till you come saying you need more."

Ruben gave a half smile at the sheriff's joking.

They were almost there.

"Why so quiet?" Crystal Gilbert asked, at last. "I figured you'd be excited to getting in to town."

"Oh, I just was thinking about what you were talking about."

"What's that?"

"About the young man who's going to help us find Carla Adkins."

"Oh, yes."

"What if he was already a lawman?"

"What about it?"

"How could he get the honorary star?"

"Why, we'd just give it to him, Ruben," the sheriff said. "We'd just order him one and present it anyway. At the banquet. That's the only way he'd get a star he could keep, you know."

"How's that?"

"Why, that star you're wearing and the badge I've got belong to the state. We have to give them back in when we retire."

"Oh."

There was a sudden light spring to the truck, as if a weight had just been lifted from the bed.

* * *

Crystal Gilbert showed Ruben where to put his clothes. "That's your drawer," he said, pointing to a small pine chest in the corner. "The one on top. The wife cleaned it out this morning."

Ruben turned his back to the sheriff and slid into the newspaper-lined drawer his clean underwear, handkerchiefs and socks. Then he laid down a neatly folded sweater, a pair of trousers, an ironed dress shirt. He was glad he'd had clean clothes at Colby Chaser's. He was glad Hilda had kept bringing them to him.

"That's your cot," Crystal motioned. "The one with the chenille spread on it."

Ruben sat down on the cot and clumsily fiddled with his shoelaces. The new shoes hurt; he missed his cowboy boots.

Crystal was going through the stack of mail on his desk.

"Nothing," he said, tossing some advertisements into the waste can. "Nothing. Just junk."

Ruben stared about him uncomfortably, adjusting to the strange format of cells stretching beyond the heavy barred door, and men yawning restlessly inside them; the odd arrangement of big, clumsy pieces of furniture; the sheriff's cluttered rolltop desk. He saw there were no guns on the wall racks.

"I'm hungry," Crystal sighed. "How about you?"

"I reckon."

"I guess we missed lunch. I could use a real good meal," Crystal added. "How about me taking you to an early dinner? Since it's your first night in town. I could sort of show you around."

Ruben stood up, pressing out the wrinkles in his shirt and trousers.

"Oh, you look fine, boy." Crystal slicked back his hair and reached for his jacket. "You look like a real deputy."

They locked the door behind him, shutting in the jailbirds' groans and yawns. "Just a bunch of drunks sleeping it off," Crystal said as he led the way down the sidewalk and across the street to Sherry's Diner. He had seen the

122

look of fear and uncertainty on the boy's face. Then the orange neon sign, flashing on and off, caught Ruben's attention. He stood for a moment, closing one eye and then the other, watching the stretched-out orange flicker in the blue afternoon air.

"It's pretty," Crystal said.

Ruben followed him through the door, waiting while he took off his jacket and hung it on the wooden rack by the candy counter.

"Don't you want to take yours off?"

"No." Ruben pulled at the pretty new jacket. He wanted to keep it on.

The sheriff chose a booth at the side of the restaurant, one with a little machine for choosing records to play. He put a nickel in and punched a button. A noisy record came on. Crystal thumped his feet on the floor and drank the glass of ice water a waitress brought him.

"What's good tonight?" he asked, after telling the girl good evening.

"Spareribs."

"Plenty of sauce?"

"Yes, sir!"

"Fine. Two orders, then."

"Vegetables?"

"What've you got?"

"Mashed potatoes and string beans."

"OK."

"Salad?"

"Yes."

"Green or gelatin?"

"Green. With Thousand Island dressing."

"Two?"

"That all right with you, Ruben?"

Ruben found that he was choked for words. He licked his lips and shook his head yes.

"What to drink?"

"Coffee."

"You, too?" the waitress asked, nodding at Ruben.

This time he could spit out yes.

"Who's your friend, Sheriff?" the waitress asked when she brought their plates.

"This here is Deputy Lawson," Crystal Gilbert said matter-of-factly.

"Oh."

"Ruben, this is Sherry."

"Pleased to meet you," the waitress said, sticking out a hip as she turned to meet him.

"Me, too," Ruben muttered.

"You new here?" she asked.

"Yes." Ruben opened and closed his mouth, staring at the table.

"Well, good to see you. Do you take cream in your coffee?" She shook her hips again as she reached to the table behind her for the cream and sugar.

"No."

"Just black, huh?"

"Yes."

"Okeydokey."

A pause. She went away. Then, "Here you are." She set down the cup, leaning over close to Ruben. He could smell the perfume in her black, curly hair.

He did not look up until she had gone.

The sheriff was smiling.

"See, boy," he said. "I told you it wouldn't be long until you'd meet a nice young girl. Next thing I know, you'll be asking me for money to take her to the pictures."

Ruben said nothing. He picked up his knife and fork and tried to eat when the food came. Crystal Gilbert was already working away, sopping his cornbread in the thick, greasy sauce, pouring salt and pepper on his gravied potatoes. The spareribs were slick on his plate, and when Ruben swiped at them with his fork, they slid from one side to the other. Embarrassed, he left them and went to his salad and potatoes. It was all cold and gummy in his mouth.

It tasted like sawdust.

The booth seat was hard and the curved wood behind him hurt his back. The music was noisy. The sheriff had just dropped another nickel in the slot. Ruben stared at the few people sitting in booths around him and at the waitress by the cash register. They all stared back. The waitress winked and arched her body over the money machine, showing her big bosom in the tight-fitting white uniform.

He felt sick inside, nauseated, stifled. These people were closing in on him. The sheriff, saying he was sorry Ruben didn't like his supper, but maybe he was too tired to be hungry, reached across for his untouched spareribs. From the eyes at the back of his head, Ruben saw the waitress perched cockily over the candy display, ready to wink if he turned again. An old man stopped by and chatted with Crystal. Their conversation was a garble of words Ruben did not understand.

"This is Quig," the sheriff said, "our barber. Quig, Deputy Lawson."

"Good to meet you."

Ruben answered, "Same to you."

Quig prattled on, a blur against the booth back. ". . . fine young men come to town to serve their community. Great young men. Proud to be living in such a fine place. . . . Great to be alive." He patted Ruben on the shoulder. "Come by for a free haircut," he said. "It's all I can do for you, boy. Drop in tomorrow. I won't be very busy then . . ."

Ruben thanked him.

Quig finally went away. Ruben could eat no more. He stared dizzily at the sheriff's thick slab of apple pie topped with ice cream, and his fresh cup of hot coffee. He thought only of his bare feet on slick, green, fresh-smelling grass, and no one around to watch him coming and going, no one to talk to him and be talked back to. His stomach tied in knots, and his eyes drooped, hiding him from the intense, prying eyes of the people who came and went, stopping to speak to Sheriff Crystal Gilbert and meet the new lawman.

The waitress walked by with hot coffee, swinging her big broad hips against the tight white uniform.

"That'll be all," Crystal thanked her. "Put it on my bill, will you?" He slid fifteen cents under his dish and motioned to Ruben that he was ready.

At last, they left the diner and walked back out into the cool evening air.

That night, when he was snug in his bunk, and his tired aching body had stretched out and unraveled its kinks under the chenille spread, the violet eyes awakened him with their blinking.

Ruben stirred, and pulled the cover tighter over his head, wrapping it around his face to seal in the darkness. But the eyes came blinking through, winking, rubbing out the sleep and the blackness, flooding him with their violet glow.

"What is it?" Ruben asked himself.

"Time," whispered the little voice inside. "Time."

Then the violet eyes began to wink and tremble and two tears formed at their black-lashed edges.

"Don't cry," Ruben whispered. "Please."

The tears held back, throbbing against their filmy fringes.

"All right," the little voice crooned softly. "All right. But go, then. Go, it's time."

Sitting up, putting his feet down on the floor, Ruben reached for his clothes. Instead of his jeans and an old shirt, he felt his green shirt and pants, soft, new, spongy to his touch. He pulled them on carefully, so he would not tear or soil them.

He was aware of the eyes flooding the room with violet, star-shaped light, brilliant enough for him to make out the sleeping, snoring form of Crystal Gilbert on his bunk against the north wall.

The heavy new shoes made a clop-clopping on the floor.

"Huh," Sheriff Gilbert cried, rolling over, his hand reaching for the pistol beneath his pillow. "Huh? Who is it?"

Ruben mumbled his name.

"What is it?" The sheriff cried, sitting up.

"It's time to go," Ruben said, thinking of Hunky and wondering why he needed to speak.

"Sure," Crystal said. "Sure, boy." He began to dress hurriedly, throwing on whatever he had lain out when he undressed. He was unaware that he was pulling on tomorrow's clothes, his old blue business-suit trousers and the coverall jacket he always wore in town.

Ruben stood, waiting, blinking from the violet light that was making him dizzy. He swayed and leaned, caught himself on the file cabinet.

"Sit down," Crystal said. "While I get the gear together." Ruben sat.

Then Crystal Gilbert guided the boy out through the rain, into the truck. Pulling on an old plastic hat and a yellow raincoat, he packed the bed of the truck with rope, boots, lanterns and shovels. He slid under the steering wheel, pushing the boy over on the seat, and began to drive out towards the East Fork.

"You just say when," Crystal said.

"All right." The boy remained silent, exhausted, threshing about quietly as he peered through the window of the truck into the black, stormy, starless night that was pulling them on towards Passerman's Hollow.

When the violet eyes grew large and round again, and the two tears in their corners welled up and puckered beneath the swollen lids, Ruben raised his hands to shut off their image and whispered aloud, "Please, don't cry."

"No," the sheriff said gently, "don't cry."

Ruben fell back against the seat and snuggled himself up against the damp slickness of the sheriff's raincoat. The bright yellow sleeve slid around his body, and hugged him closer.

"Can I have a raincoat?" Ruben asked.

"You bet," Sheriff Gilbert said.

"Where is it?"

"Under the seat."

Ruben reached under and pulled out the slicker.

"Pretty," he said, stroking it. "Pretty." He pulled it over him and looked out the window from his safe, plastic-protected world within the truck. Night birds wore yellow plastic raincoats in a storm. Hadn't he always known that? It made them look like golden-haired day birds flying through the warm summer air, flying, circling, flying on, looking for a place to light.

The rains beat down (how long had they been coming?) and the creeks gnashing away at their sodden banks beat their way through at last and raced down the slimy-surfaced fields. They ran and they ran, angry and destructive, like half-clothed specters let loose from imaginary prisms of wall that had held them back. First the thaw, and now a flash flood. Dragging branches and grasses and clumps of pulverized earth, the creeks swept first to right, then to left, finding furrows to flow down, finding hollows to surge down, finding any weak thing that would give way to their staggering force.

Swearing to himself, Crystal slowed the truck, hitting the clutch easy so he would not slide. He pumped the brake slowly and sat behind the wheel, shaking his head. They could not cross the bridge at the foot of the hill. But they had to.

The boy was waiting, watching him. Letting his breath whistle out between his teeth as he made up his mind, Crystal parked the pickup where he had stopped, then drew on his hip boots, grunting as he swung his body from one side to the other and tugged at the tough slippery boot tops. He watched Ruben grope for the tops of his, imitating each movement the sheriff made as he pulled, steadied and fastened the rubbers about his thick legs.

Then Ruben fell back against the seat, panting.

"You're just all wore out, boy, aren't you?" the sheriff asked.

Ruben nodded fretfully.

"All wore out."

Then Crystal pulled the boy out of the truck and gave him a lantern to carry. Crystal took a length of rope, a shovel and another lantern. He pushed Ruben in front of him, and watched him leap the creek, clumsy from the weight of the stiff, cumbersome clothing he was unused to. He jumped heavily and landed on his hands and knees, dropping the lantern in front of him. Crystal followed, fording the stream easily, his big weight an anchor that met the mad rush of the creek with equal force.

"Come on, boy," he helped Ruben to his feet and pushed him on again. He followed, feeling his way along on the soggy ground, struggling to maintain his balance and keep pace with the boy. The shovel, bearing down hard on his shoulders, made his body ache. The lantern light was feeble and spotty, casting freckles on the turning, heaving ground. Rain spit in his face, and the grassiness beneath him gave way with each step.

But Crystal went on, following the boy who found the path that led to Passerman's Hollow.

Ruben led the sheriff up the twisting cowpath, once a living trail busy with the footsteps of children playing or coming home from school the long way or just chasing in the cattle, now a thing of death and destruction in the maze of rain and hail that slashed at it ferociously.

Crystal walked carefully, each step a well-placed plod for fear the bank would give way beneath his weight and carry him into a swimming sea of mud and slosh.

Ruben led the sheriff to the plot where he had lain and cried the day that Hunky Miller had sat in the pawpaw tree and watched over him. He pointed to the empty, belching, jagged rip in the earth that had already torn loose and riveted its way down the hollow, following the course of the stream.

Crystal nodded, throwing down his shovel. He wouldn't need it now, and he wouldn't carry it back to the pickup. He would leave it, as a marker, and hope that the rains, having done their destruction here, would not wash it away.

Ruben let out a tired, empty, little cry and looked at the sheriff.

Crystal Gilbert opened his mouth to speak, to say something to the boy, but nothing would come out but saliva flooded with rain and the great tears flushing down his drawn face.

Then Ruben, seeing lightning come crashing through the treetops, threw himself into Crystal's arms, trembling, wild with fear. The sheriff, not expecting the weight of the boy to fly into his chest, stumbled backwards, tripped over a fallen tree branch and went rolling down the hill, still clutching his lantern tightly in his hand.

Ruben covered his head with his hands to shut out the oncoming brilliance of the violet streaks of laughter. He cried out and pushed backwards, but they came on, dazzling him with their metallic lunges through the black night, breaking open paths of sheared-off trees and falling debris.

Then he fell, too, snarled by the razor sharpness of a vein of yellow lightning that had lodged its fury against the tin star on his breast.

ammering on the door and shouting savagely, Crystal Gilbert awakened Phace Adkins and his wife Myra. Half drowned by the rain and the sweat of his own exertion, the sheriff staggered into the room and collapsed on the floor, releasing his limp burden in a stream of dirty water.

Phace, throwing on a robe, lit candles and a kerosene lantern, explaining in little puffs of just-caught breath that the electricity had gone off hours ago.

"Where've you been?" he asked the sheriff.

"Up the hollow," Crystal shouted to make himself heard above the roar of the thunder.

"Who's that?" Phace pointed to the bundle on the hand-hooked rug.

Crystal turned back the yellow hood and showed Phace Adkins the terror-frozen face of Ruben Lawson, seared violet by the force of the burning lightning that had struck him.

Phace dropped numbly to the floor beside the sheriff. "My God," he said. "How'd it happen?"

Crystal shook his head. "I still don't know."

Phace began to weep, and Myra, standing behind him now, a kerosene lamp in her hand and her long gown billowing up in white muslin puffs as the wind rattled through the house, asked, "Did you find my girl?"

"I found where she was," Crystal said to Phace, too tired to disguise the ugliness of the truth but not wanting to have to face Myra with it. "The rains had opened up her grave and swept her down the hollow. The place looked like it had been opened up so many times there wasn't anything left to hold it. The earth was awfully soft there, Phace," he added, lowering his voice.

But Myra had heard and, with a wild cry, she rushed towards the door, pulled it open with a sudden burst of strength, and threw herself out into the night, letting a gush of wind and rain sweep into the room, extinguish the candles and beat with hollow, wet fury upon the dead boy on the floor.

"Oh, Lord," she was crying. "Oh, dear Lord, dear God, dear Christ Jesus. Oh, Lord."

Sobbing and screaming, Phace went after her, scooting to the door on his knees as he hit back at the rain with his bare hands. Then he heaved himself up to his feet and stumbled out across the yard.

"Myra," he called, "Myra, come back. Myra!"

She stopped then, and looked back, tottering long enough for him to catch her by the arm and jerk her back towards him, slapping at her and the night in his fright and anger.

"Oh dear Lord, dear God, Christ Jesus," she sobbed again as she stood there barefooted in the rain, her head against Phace's chest, her arms around his waist, listening to him cry as he held her to him.

Crystal stood watching them from the porch where he was leaning his weight against the door to stop its banging into the wall.

"It's all right, now Myra, it's all right," Phace said at last, over and over, as he patted his wife gently, wiping the rain from her face. "It's all over now. There's no one out here who can help you. Bring your sorrow back inside."

Myra nodded between sobs and let Phace push her back towards the house. They went slowly, side by side, their bodies bent down as if in prayer to escape the sting of the savage wind and hard rain. When they reached the porch, Phace felt he could go no farther. But Crystal Gilbert was there waiting, and he understood their tiredness, and the deepness of their sorrow, as he bent and pulled them in.

They dried off the candles and lit them again.

"Here," Phace said, bringing out a bottle of whiskey

from the piano bench. He poured out a drink for the sheriff and Myra. Then he took one himself.

The two men said nothing, as they shook their bodies to rid them of the dirt and wet and evil that seemed lodged against their very bones.

Then Crystal Gilbert said, "I've got to go up the hill."

"With the boy?" Phace asked.

"Yes."

"Can't it wait?" Myra asked in a quavering voice.

"I can't let it," Crystal said. "I can't stand it until morning."

"All right," Phace mumbled. "I'll come with you. You might need help."

"I don't want to be alone," Myra cried.

"You'll be all right," Phace told her. "There's nothing can harm you now."

The storm awakened her, aroused her, and Hilda Lawson lay threshing in her bed, afraid that the evil-tempered winds would suck out the child that was growing in her belly.

Mason was awake, too, pawing at her gently, trying to comfort her.

When she wrenched herself away and snapped at him to leave her be, he lit the lamp they kept by their bed for such emergencies and began to read from the Bible. He read aloud until Hilda told him to give her some quiet, if he could do nothing else for her.

Hurt and stung, Mason looked at his wife from big eyes flooding with tears.

"Hilda?" he begged. "Hilda, why? Why not God's word on a night like this?"

"Because," she snarled, "it's not God's night. It's the devil's night out there—can't you tell? And there's evil on the wind, and evil in the grass, and no room for good." Then she held to her aching body and groaned.

When I looked for good, then evil came unto me: and when I waited for light, there came darkness.

"God's word," Mason said calmly, "can drive out the evil from your heart, and your heart can drive it from the world."

"No," Hilda said, putting her face up close to his and fixing him with her glimmering eyes. "No, Mason. God's word does nothing, nothing do you hear? Nothing but anger the devil. And he's mad enough!"

She sat up, ripping loose her gown, pulling at the braids that were unwound from her restlessness. Then she threw back the cover and lay there, on the top of the sheet, her nakedness exposed as a kind of altar for whatever ritual evil the devil needed an altar to perform on.

Mason, horrified, shrank to his side of the bed and stared at this woman. Where was his Hilda, the shy, modest, God-fearing woman he had married and lived with, the woman who had been critical of him and harsh at times, but never raving and shameless and godless?

How that they told you there should be mockers in the last time, who should walk after their own ungodly lusts. These be they who separate themselves, sensual, having not the Spirit.

"Can't you hear it?" she mumbled. "Can't you hear it coming?"

"What?" Mason asked. He inched over towards Hilda. "What's coming?"

"You know," she whispered.

Whether it be good, or whether it be evil, we will obey the voice of the Lord our God, to whom we send thee . . .

Mason, trembling, tried to stroke her cheek, as the lightning flashed and lit up the house with a wave of purple iridescence.

Bristol and Griffith came tottering down the hall, knocking at the door, begging to be let in. Clumsily, Mason covered his wife with her gown and called to them. The little boys, frightened, climbed into the bed with their parents and huddled against what warmth they could find.

"Where's Rebecca?" Mason asked.

"In her room," Griffith said. "She's sitting up in bed with a candle lit."

"She didn't want to come," Bristol said. "We asked her, but she didn't want to come."

Over an hour later, when the sheriff knocked on the door, it was Hilda Lawson who slipped away from her sleeping husband and children, threw on robe and slippers and went down the stairs, a candle in her hand, to see who wanted in from the storm.

"Crystal Gilbert," the sheriff called.

"Who's that with you?"

"Phace Adkins."

"Come in."

The two men stomped inside, scraping their boots as best they could on the waterlogged floor.

"We've brought you your boy, Mrs. Mason," Sheriff Gilbert said. "We've left him outside in the truck." His voice was tired, his face was tired, and he could not soften his words. "He's dead."

Hilda, one hand over her stomach, felt the candle tremble in her hand. Then, straightening up and remembering the life within her, she steadied the light and went to see about a lamp.

"You'd better tell me first," Mason Lawson said from the top of the stairs.

"I will, Mason. I'll tell you what I know tonight, but I've not pieced everything together in my mind. The one thing I'd like to do is speak to your girl Rebecca."

"No," Hilda said firmly.

"Just for a minute, Mrs. Mason. Then I'll go."

"No."

"Come on, Sheriff," Mason said. "She's up here."

135

Phace Adkins followed the sheriff up the stairs and Mason Lawson led the way down the pine hall. Hilda hesitated, then went along behind. She had folded her robe heavily over her stomach, as if to keep the new child within her from hearing what was going to be told in the room upstairs.

What, my son? And what, the son of my womb? And what, the son of my vows?

Mason checked to make sure Bristol and Griffith were asleep in his big bed before he took the sheriff and Phace Adkins into Becky's room.

"Becky?" he called. "Becky?"

There was darkness and no sound of breathing.

"Hilda, shine your light in here," Mason called.

Hilda stepped over the threshold of the room and held her candle up high. The bed was empty. Mason stopped and looked beneath it, then opened the closet and felt behind Rebecca's clothes.

"No one," he said. Fright in his eyes, he ran from room to room calling "Rebecca! Rebecca!" Hilda close behind him.

Bristol, sleepy eyed, raised up when his father shined the light in his eyes.

"I told you, Pa," he said. "She's in her room with the candle lit." Then he went back to sleep.

Mason Lawson and Crystal Gilbert stared at each other.

When the knocking came on the door, Rebecca heard Hunky Miller's whistle. She waited for Ruben to slip into her room. But he did not come. Then, when Hunky whistled again, and after her parents went downstairs, she went into the room where Ruben had stayed and took down the boards from the window.

Hunky motioned for her to come down.

She slipped through the window and anchored on the stoop of the back porch. Hunky swung himself up the porch posts and helped her drop down into the grass.

She held her gown around her closer and looked into Hunky's frightened face.

"What is it?" she asked. "What's wrong?"

Hunky shook his head and spluttered. He tried using signals with her, as he did with Ruben when he was too excited to speak clearly.

Rebecca took his hands in hers and smiled calmly and said, "You'll have to tell me, Hunky."

He nodded and led Rebecca into the smokehouse where they would be sheltered from the storm.

"Ruben's dead," he gasped, at last.

Rebecca's face went white, her thin body shook, and she collapsed against Hunky, trembling.

"When?" she panted.

"Just now—"

"Who came to the house?"

"Sheriff Gilbert and Phace Adkins."

"Did they bring Ruben?"

Hunky nodded.

"Do you know what happened?"

Hunky looked at the little girl and smiled. "I know," he said.

"Tell me," she begged.

"For a kiss."

"All right." Crouching over Hunky, the outlines of her wet body showing through her soaked gown, she kissed him gently on the cheek. Hunky smiled happily and moved away.

"Ruben took Sheriff Gilbert to Passerman's Hollow," he said, clipping his words short.

"Where?"

"Where you found us last Saturday, when you were with Bristol and Griffith."

Rebecca nodded. "Why'd he go?"

"Sheriff promised reward—money, pictures, star to man who helped him find Carla."

"Did they find Carla?"

"No."

"How come?"

"Creeks got there first. Washed away."

"What happened to Ruben?"

Hunky made motions of lightning with his right hand.

"How'd you know about this, Hunky?"

Hunky smiled. "I always know," he said.

"I mean, about tonight."

Hunky smiled again and shook his head.

"Tell me, Hunky," Rebecca leaned towards the stooped-over little man. "Tell me what happened to Carla."

Hunky shook his head.

"Why?"

"I promised I'd never tell."

"Who'd you promise?"

Hunky's lips trembled then were still.

"Was it Ruben?"

"I promised Ruben; Ruben promised me."

"Tell me, Hunky," Rebecca was so close that her breath was hot on Hunky's face and her small round breasts pressed against his chest. "Tell me. Did you call to her when she was going down the steps to the church basement? Did you call her out in the yard and tell her Ruben was waiting for her?"

Hunky, frightened, drew back, flattening himself against the wall.

"You took her to Passerman's Hollow," Rebecca cried. "But did you kill her? Or keep her there for Ruben?"

Hunky trembled and shook his stallion head. He was afraid of this girl with angry eyes and breath and hot, hard body that pinned him to the wall. But he was more afraid to move against her because Ruben had threatened him, had threatened to kill him if he ever touched her the way he had touched Carla. And now he was more afraid of Ruben's ghost than he had been of Ruben's body. He had been able to watch Ruben alive, but Ruben's ghost was everywhere, hiding in the flowers, lurking under the trees, maybe even in the empty boxes over there against the wall.

"I know about the note Ruben wrote her," Rebecca said. "I got it from her on the bus. I know that Ruben was going to meet her at Friday-night church. But you knew, too, didn't you, Hunky? You knew that Ruben wrote that note because you put it in her locker! And you knew what it said!"

Letting loose a caged animal's cry, Hunky sprang up and dashed out the smokehouse door, down the hill, slipping through the water and mud and rubble of fallen trees as he made his way home towards Moonridge and Colby Chaser.

But in the slicky meadow grass, his heart throbbing from fear and anger, his eyes blinded by the blackness of the rain-slashed night, Hunky stopped. His heart thumped, his body coarsened, his brain spun. Ahead, through narrow slit eyes, he saw the house, warm and dry, waiting for him. To his right, down the tramped-out path, was Passerman's Hollow, nestled in its cache of thick darkness. For a moment he was uncertain. Then, his decision was made. With a snort and a spin of his slippery feet, Hunky threw back his head and began to run.

Rebecca sat in the hall closet, crouched up for warmth beneath an old dress of her mother's. She heard her father calling for her through the house. They still had not gone to the pickup truck. They were looking for her before they did that. She saw flashes as the kerosene lamps were lit. She heard the sounds of steps and the slamming of the kitchen door.

But when the steps grew nearer, she flattened out against the wall until she could crouch behind the boxes, covering herself with the dress. She waited until her father had shined in the light, until he and Phace Adkins and Crystal Gilbert had gone on towards the tool shed, talking excitedly and with loud voices. She didn't want them to find her yet. She had to be by herself first and think it out inside her head. She had to *be* Ruben one last time, and to know *why*.

The footsteps of the men faded and Rebecca slipped out into the hall and into Ruben's room again. She stood where she had so often let herself out through his window, and once she moved to make the slide to the kitchen stoop. Then she stopped. There was no need to go. She knew now what would be waiting in Passerman's Hollow, and she knew that her place was here at home, protecting what was left of Ruben's memory, looking after Bristol and Griffith, comforting Carla's mother. And she *understood,* at last, why things had had to happen this way—because Ruben was what he was, and no one could ever have changed him or the way he saw the world.

She leaned her face from the window just long enough to catch her breath and let the rain wash away the tears from her face.

"Oh, Ruben," she whispered, knowing it was the last time she would ever speak to him this way. "Oh, Ruben, why couldn't you have come back for me? I could have helped you. Maybe I could even have saved you, if I'd known. Oh, Ruben, why did you have to do it this way? Why did you want the star?"

She pulled herself back from the window, then, and walked across the room to the door. Just once she looked back towards the empty rollaway.

"Oh, Ruben, Ruben," she said. "Why were you the way you were? You told for the star, but you wouldn't tell for me."

Then she opened the door and started quietly down the stairs.

Sheriff Gilbert and his men wasted no time in getting to Passerman's Hollow the next morning. They went in big-wheeled trucks, loaded with boots, raincoats, lanterns, ropes, picks and shovels. They took thermos bottles of hot coffee, a quart of buttermilk and a big hamper of cake and cheese sandwiches. They carried blankets and sleeping bags. They came with the first light, and they were prepared to stay until they had done their job.

But they didn't stay long.

Morning, with its cutting clearness and bright, transparent light, showed them that their work was already done. At the bottom of the hollow, where the debris forced down by the night's storm had lodged against tree trunks and heavy trussed rocks, was the body of Carla Adkins, washed up at the foot of a slender tree.

Carla's arms were thrown sideways, her head was tilted back, and her open violet eyes stared up, as if in horror, to the branch from which Hunky Miller was suspended by the belt from his blue-denim jeans, the half smile frozen on his face, his turned down eyes staring through them all as he swung back and forth, back and forth, gently in the wind.